The Body Farm: A Novella

by Brian Martinez

Introduction

Hello, human.

The Body Farm is a story that took on a life of its own, if you'll forgive the pun. Originally posted online as a one-part story, readers enjoyed it so much that I was inspired to expand it further and further, until it took on the ten-part form you see before you. It has made appearances on a handful of creepypasta sites, and even been adapted to audio by several narrators, most notably Jason Hill, of Chilling Tales for Dark Nights and Horror Hill. To date it's one of my most popular stories, which is funny considering I'd never intended to write it. It just goes to show you, you never know what will die, and what will live.

Special thanks go to Craig Groshek, creator and runner of the Simply Scary Podcasts Network, for taking a liking to my weird little story and broadcasting it much further than it ever would have gone otherwise. If you like listening to horror stories, you really owe it to yourself to check out his fantastic podcasts and Youtube channels.

Included here are The Depths and Lungflower, two stories I'm particularly proud of. Both have a more introspective feel to them than The Body Farm, and I think as such they make a nice counterpoint.

As always thanks for reading. If you want to reach out to me with any comments, criticisms, condescensions, promises, prognostications or proclamations, you can always send an email to brian@bloodstreamcity.com and I'll do my best to answer every one of them.

Sincerely,
Brian Martinez

The Depths

We sailed south from Japan. The ocean was angry at the beginning of our voyage, spitting and smashing at us for most of the eleven-hundred miles. As we moved closer, the raging waters drew still. Quiet. Like a married couple on the verge of a fight. Rage bubbling beneath the skin.

Our destination was an abyss. Not a bottomless pit, exactly, but not far from it.

***

The Mariana Trench was first discovered by rope. Picture that. It's 1875, you're on board the HMS Challenger, a steam-assisted boat making a scientific tour of the world. You're around a hundred miles out from the Mariana Islands, recording data in your notebook. Your crew has already discovered four-thousand some-odd previously unknown species of aquatic life, enough to make your head spin. During a routine sounding of the ocean floor, using nothing more than weighted ropes, your rope begins to drop. And drop. And drop. And it doesn't stop dropping until it reaches a measurement of eight thousand, one hundred and eighty-four meters. An impossible depth. You're so confused you do it all over again. And you get the same reading.

Eight thousand, one hundred and eighty-four meters. That's seven miles, straight down. Drop a pebble from the surface and it would take an hour just to reach bottom. Drop Mount Everest and, after the water settled, the peak of Earth's tallest mountain would still be a full mile beneath you.

"How deep is the ocean?" The joke goes.

"You couldn't possibly fathom."

The Mariana Trench is a scar. A crescent-shaped scratch in the Earth's crust.

One I planned to touch.

***

People were excited by the idea of the first woman to dive the Mariana Trench. The very first to reach the deepest point of the world's oceans. Half a dozen men had made the dive already, they said, it was time for a woman to join them. Rewrite the history books. I went along with the story for the sake of funding, because donors love a good news story. But the truth is, I've never thought of myself in that way. I'm not a woman. I'm a diver. An explorer.

I didn't want to get my name into the history books- I just wanted to go down there for myself.

To sit at the bottom of the world.

Our boat was called the Leucothea, named after the Greek sea goddess. Leucothea was said to come to the aid of sailors in trouble. Ours was a research vessel, built in the eighties. Just like me. Made one for one purpose only.

Just like me.

It wasn't the newest or the most advanced ship on the ocean, and that was just fine. It doesn't take the best ship in the world, it just takes one that doesn't stop before you get there. There was one thing we had that was the best in the world, though. Where it counted.

Our dive vessel was one-of-a-kind. The smallest and lightest craft of its type, built on the backs of all the successes and failures that came before it. A Vanadium-steel oval with mechanical limbs. The development team nicknamed it Sheldon, on account of it looking like an egg with legs. When it came time to name it officially, however, I christened it the Palaemon.

Palaemon. Offspring of Leucothea. The child that roams the sea.

The night before the dive, I couldn't sleep. It was the depths that did it. We'd reached our destination late and decided to wait for daybreak. It didn't matter below the surface, but up on deck it made things easier. The problem was, with the Leucothea drifting over the trench, I could only lie in my quarters, on that hard cot, and imagine the seven miles stretching out beneath me. The cold space under my back.

All that darkness. Waiting for me down there. Calling to me.

I needed to rest, to have my wits about me on the dive, but I couldn't take anything to help me fall asleep. Nothing in my system. Clean, like a baby. Like a newly hatched egg. So I kept my eyes shut and tried not to think about the ocean. About anything at all. I let my mind go blank, trying in vain to keep the pressure from crushing in.

Before I knew it, before I could stop it, I was standing in front of the Palaemon, the cold metal of the dive floor stinging my bare feet. Wishing I'd at least stopped for socks. But stopping wasn't in my design.

At least the Palaemon was resting. Limbs folded against its body, the cameras like six, dead eyes staring out at peculiar angles, it sat at the center of the dive floor. We would come together as one soon, the machine and I. Falling through cold space. Piercing the black. I placed my hand on the hatch and said a small, godless prayer under my breath that we would reach the bottom.

"It really does look like an egg," a voice said behind me. I turned to see John, head of the dive project, watching me from the railing. Salt-bleached hair caught in the light.

"Better an egg than a coffin."

He padded down the metal steps and joined me in front of the Palaemon. His dirty socks next to my bare feet. We looked at each other a moment. "I couldn't sleep, either," he said. I nodded, nothing more to be said. "Radar shows a storm moving in."

"I saw that." Swirls of green with a red core, less than a day out. A vague monster on the horizon in shifting shades of violence.

"But you still want to dive."

I nodded. "I still want to dive."

John knew how much I wanted this. He wanted it, too, but he had the misfortune of being the voice of reason to someone who didn't want to hear it. Which was why he was stepping so lightly, socks and all. "If the weather's as bad as they say, it might be too risky to move forward. We have to at least consider it."

"I won't be feeling much of anything at the bottom."

"You do have to come back up eventually," he said with a frown. "Or hadn't you thought of that?"

"I considered it."

"And?"

"The truth?" I looked over at him. "I just want to get out of here already."

"Is it something I said?" He asked, and I laughed softly. "Ava, just tell me the truth- are you running from me?"

I turned and walked away from John and the Palaemon. Two children of the sea. "No," I said, heading back to my quarters. "Not from you."

The floor was either warmer on the way back or I couldn't feel it anymore. As for my bed, I don't remember my head hitting the pillow. The darkness drew me in like a sponge.

***

I sat inside an egg. A circle of lights and instruments, with me at the yolk. The Palaemon, a steel-alloy ball dangling a few feet over the ocean. A pebble waiting to be dropped.

"Palaemon, this is Leucothea. How's it going in there?" John's voice came in strong over the radio.

"I haven't gone anywhere yet."

"Jesus, Ava, just give me a damn reading, would you?" I read off the numbers to him and he confirmed them. All systems running perfectly. The ocean spray hit the pilot window again and again as the Palaemon swayed, dangling from six suspension cables.

I've always had a strong stomach, but even for me, that much back-and-forth was enough to induce vertigo. This was no time for getting sick, so I focused on the mission. The controls in front of me. The multi-million dollar machine I was entrusting with my life.

Over my head was a saltwater battery. Above that an antenna array and a beacon light. Behind me, horizontal and vertical thrusters. A thousand instruments packed in with me, like the antennae of snail, touching and testing its surroundings. Warning me of danger.

"Alright, it looks like we're clear. Palaemon, brace for impact in ten seconds," John said, and just like that the countdown started.

"Ten, nine, eight..."

I tucked my head down and held my knees in the fetal position.

"Seven, six, five..."

For no reason at all, I thought of my brother.

"Four..."

Blonde and small and bright.

"Three..."

How he liked to play in the mud.

"Two..."

I wondered what he would have looked like today.

"One, releasing cables."

For a second, nothing happened. Then, like a gunshot, the pins holding the suspension cables fired. All at once they let go, and all was weightless. All was light. An endless moment floating on the air. The embryo and the egg.

Then the ocean rushed up at the pilot window like a runaway truck. A splash like an explosion blotted out the light as the water enveloped me, pulled me down and down into the hungry water.

We dropped, the Palaemon and I, taking the same path as that weighted rope all those years ago. The sea was a greenish-blue expanse that grew darker and darker through the window, bubbles dissipating until all that was left was the whisper of water rushing past. An occasional fish caught in the lights. We passed the thousand meter mark in no time, falling down to where the sunlight doesn't reach.

The Aphotic Zone. Greek for away from light.

We fell. And fell. And kept falling. I kept in contact with the Leucothea at first, but soon there was nothing to say that silence wouldn't say better.

Somewhere around five-thousand feet, fifteen-hundred meters down, I passed into the Mariana Trench.

Not that I could see it, of course. The trench is forty-three miles wide at most parts, which means the Palaemon's lights were about as useful as a match in a tornado. I fell for more than hour, watching the screens, occasionally checking to make sure the radio worked, to let the surface know I was alive. It felt as if I could fall forever. Some part of me wished I could.

I was mostly alone as I fell. Occasionally I saw a Snailfish, the elongated fish with small eyes in their heads and antifreeze in their blood. I even spotted what looked like a Ghost fish, the elusive, scaleless fish with translucent skin and colorless eyes, but it passed by too quickly to be sure.

Then there was nothing. The temperature outside read thirty-nine degrees Fahrenheit, the warmest it gets down there. The barometer showed a thousand times Earth's atmosphere. At that pressure, if were I to open the hatch, I would be crushed faster than my brain could register the pain. The Palaemon was a sphere because it was the strongest shape for resisting pressure, yet by then it had shrunken by two inches under the immense pressure.

The first screen to flicker was a secondary system, camera control. It cut out, the screen gone black. Then the speed and depth monitor shimmered in digital. "Leucothea," I said into the radio, "this is Palaemon, can you still read me? Over." Five seconds passed in silence. Six seconds. Seven. I turned up the volume.

"-cutting out, over." John's voice jumped through the speaker.

"Same here. I'm losing a few minor systems. Nothing catastrophic. Over." The image on the main screen wobbled. The life support monitor blinked an early warning.

"If...can't let..." The radio signal cut in and out, John's voice sliced to pieces. "...weather is-"

And then there was nothing. No more voice from the radio. I was alone, with one screen to guide me, and less than a thousand meters to go before the bottom. We'd have to figure out later why I'd lost so many systems, but for now I had what I needed. Air was flowing, the cockpit was holding up to the pressure, the controls were functional, and the lights still worked, both the ambient lights already on and the flood lights I'd kept off to conserve battery. For the first time, I engaged reverse thrusters to slow my descent.

Five hundred meters until the bottom. Four hundred meters. Three. I leaned forward, until my face was nearly touching the pilot window, and strained to see. I felt like a little girl on a field trip to the zoo. Wide-eyed, peering out from the bus windows at the creatures peering back.

My eyes registered a thin line in the darkness below. A trace of something solid. As the Palaemon neared the bottom, less than a hundred meters to go, I flicked on the flood lights.

The house below looked like the one I'd grown up in. A tall roof with gray shingles, now ringed with mossy growth. The flood lights caught the brick chimney. It threw a harsh shadow across the roof and down to the ocean floor. Lichen clung to the chimney's old brick. An Amphipod swam off, a massive, soft-shelled albino disturbed from its feeding.

I piloted the mostly-blind Leucothea across the sloping roof and down toward the trench's floor. The flood light danced across the attached garage and its faded red door with white panels. Inside would be a brown station wagon, and a yellow bicycle with a cracked seat. A workbench covered in rusted tools and half-finished birdhouses.

Carefully turning the stick, I slowly touched down on the Mariana's floor. Contact. Sediment billowed up around me in slow motion. Like playing in the mud. Even there, that far down, things lived in the dirt. Xenophyophores, unicellular organisms hidden in the sand and sediment. Microbes in the muck.

The house was silent in the water, bathed in the Palaemon's light. Marine snow drifted across the roof and down to the open porch. A Trachymedusa jellyfish, a translucent, umbrella-shaped phantom, pulsed through the water, swimming past the picture window.

Past the face inside.

My mother's soft cheekbones looked angular in the light. Straight hair swept sideways in the soft current. Red lips like a soft scar.

"Ava."

Her dress was simple and light and the color of seaweed. She lifted her thin arms. Her long hands stretched toward me.

"Ava."

I understood then. Understood what she needed. What I needed. My hands found the pilot door, fingers working the locking mechanism. I couldn't be trapped in there any longer. Away from her. I needed to be with her. In my house. Where I belong.

"Palaemon, this is Leucothea, do you copy?"

A voice jarred me. Cut through the fog of radio and ocean.

"Ava, please respond."

I looked back at the radio. At the door mechanism in my hands. At the water waiting to rush in. Faster than my brain could register the pain.

"I'm not sure if you can hear me. The storm is getting close now. We need to wrap up and head back. Over."

My mother's eyes were hollow, empty. A place I could move in and make whole. They could do the same for me. For my eyes. For the hollowness that sits in me. Playing in the mud.

"If you can hear me, please come back," John's voice said.

I pulled myself from the window and returned to the pilot's seat. There were no screens left. I had no visible commands, only a stick and a lever. A lever with one word written on it in white letters.

Ascend.

"Ava. Come back."

I closed my eyes and pulled the lever. Faster than the pain could register. With a mechanical whine the Palaemon let go of its two, three-hundred kilogram weights. Released from its burden, the craft lifted free of the ocean floor.

I opened my eyes. Already heading up. I looked down at the house, at the picture window half-obscured by falling snow. My mother stared up at me. Watched me go. Watched me leave her.

The radio was solid in my hand. An anchor. A tether to the world. "I copy you, Leucothea," I said into it. "I'm coming back to you."

Like a rocket I rose. Like a bat out of hell.

***

Everyone was disappointed to learn the cameras failed, not a second of footage taken past the freefall. But the sensors recorded everything, including the depths. Eight thousand, one hundred and eighty-four meters. Seven miles, straight down. They popped their champagne and smiled for cameras. The donors were happy. The history books rewritten.

I didn't tell them about what I saw. Not any of them, not even John. But since we got back, since we returned to the land and the noisy world that went with it, I've thought of one thing and one thing only. Of going back down to the depths.

To see her.

To go home.

***

Lungflower

He was alone, but it hadn't always been that way. He'd almost had a wife once.

Victor lived in the last house on a dead end street. After he proposed to Iris, his high school sweetheart and still the most beautiful woman he'd ever met, he used his life savings to buy an old house in an old neighborhood.

The house was eighty years old. The roof sagged, mice ran behind the walls, half the electrical sockets were dead and it smelled of mildew, but he loved it. He loved it because it was theirs. Whenever he had the money, he put it into the house. Fixed it up, one room at a time. First he painted and patched what was needed. Then he added a gazebo. Then an extra bedroom. It grew like a vine, imperfect but gradual progress, twisting and stretching toward the sun.

He told Iris the new bedroom would make a perfect nursery. The light was just perfect. He should have taken the look on her face as a sign, but Victor was blinded by the future. He spent so much time staring into it, it left spots in his vision. Like all sunspots, they eventually became blindspots.

"You're distant" she told him one day.

"I'm right here," he said, looking through a catalog.

"You are, but you aren't."

He didn't understand what she meant, so he didn't take her seriously. She continued to tell him he was distant, sometimes at home, sometimes while they were at the store or in the car, or on the phone at work, until one night she told him she needed space.

Victor begged her to stay. He offered to sleep in the new bedroom. He'd give her all the space she wanted, time to figure things out. She packed her bags and left the next morning.

As he watched her pull away, out of the driveway he hadn't had the money to fix yet, he was struck with a sudden coughing fit. He'd never coughed like this before. It felt as if his lungs were filled up with thistles.

The cough worsened over the coming days. People at the office were annoyed by it, the constant sound, but he couldn't do anything about it. Medicine didn't work. Tea didn't work. Honey didn't work. The more he tried to stop coughing, the worse it became. People told him to go to the doctor, but he didn't listen. They didn't know what they were talking about, and he didn't have the money to throw away on doctors.

There was still so much to be done on the house.

***

The days went on. Life moved at a crawl. Work. Home. Work. Home. Asleep. Awake. Asleep. Awake. Always tired. Always coughing.

One morning, three months after Iris had left, three months though it felt like ten years, he woke up at the usual time for work and realized he couldn't do this any longer. There was simply no point in showering. No point getting dressed. No point driving to work and sitting behind a desk and looking at all those people as they looked back at him either in pity or resentment, annoyed at his coughing.

There was no point in any of it anymore. It had taken him three months to see it, but now that he did, it was so clear. There was nothing left.

It took everything Victor had in him to get out of the big, empty bed, shuffle down the long, empty hallway and into the cold, empty bathroom. He coughed the entire way, the wet sound echoing off old walls, walls newly-painted to cover up the stains and the mold spots. The carpet under his feet hiding the worn-down flooring.

Victor looked at himself in the mirror above the leaky sink. The sad, tired man looked back at him. But Victor didn't see this. All he saw was a cloudy mirror with dark spots on its surface, the edges going silver-black.

A faint glimmer caught Victor's eye. Something shiny on the windowsill. It was a razor blade. He'd left it there after using it to remove some old masking tape from the window. The tape had baked onto the glass over the years. Why it was there in the first place, he didn't know.

Victor picked up the blade. He turned it over, admiring the way the morning light danced on its edge. It was the nicest thing in the whole bathroom. The newest and the cleanest. The brightest thing he'd seen in months.

He looked at the razor. Looked at his wrist. The vein pumping tired blood through his tired body. He lay the blade against his skin. "I'm sorry," he said to Iris, and to the house. They were all he'd be leaving behind.

A coughing fit struck him just then, the worst yet. He coughed so hard he couldn't breathe. Blue-green stars glittered in his vision. Fingertips went numb. The razor fell from his hand and clattered under the sink. He doubled over, knees shaking, and coughed into his open hands like his soul was leaving him.

On one, final cough that felt like it came from the very center, of him, something came up. It was wet and heavy, and it slapped hard into his hand.

The coughing had stopped. He could breathe again. The stars in his eyes died and faded away. But his hand was warm. He opened it to see what was inside.

Victor had never seen a tumor before. It looked about what he expected it to look like. Pink and gray flesh gone wrong. Soft folds of abnormal growth. He should have been horrified. He should have been running to a hospital, scared for his life and begging to hear options. But he felt nothing other than a vague sense of curiosity at the the ball of flesh in the center of his palm. He looked closer, fascinated to see what his body had been busy doing while he'd been doing so little.

As Victor watched, two of its folds parted, movement too deliberate to be the simple settling of wet flesh. And then, as he continued to watch the thing in his hand, a small cry came from it.

Here was the shock. Here was the terror. Victor felt a cold ball of it in his gut. Felt his eyes go wide and his throat squeeze tight.

Horrified by the thing in his hands, Victor ran to the sink and turned the rusty faucet to full, thrusting his hands under the blast of hot water. The wet ball of tissue swirled around the old sink, pausing at the lip of the drain before the water washed it away.

For some reason he didn't understand, panic gripped him. Victor fumbled to turn off the faucet. He cut off the harsh flow of water from the spout, but it was too late. The ball of flesh tumbled down the drain, sucking down and out of sight.

Victor was horrified by what he'd done. He dropped to his knees and grabbed the pipe underneath the sink. It was thick with rust and slime, his already wet hands nearly slipping free. Victor gripped the curved sink trap as tightly as he could and unscrewed both ends, fighting the years of rust and build-up as water sprayed his face and the wall and floor. He pulled so hard the pipe nearly ripped out of the wall.

The sink trap came off. Dirty water gushed from above, spreading out along the green tile. He pulled himself closer, strained to look inside, to find what he'd flushed away.

It was gone. Gone like it had never been there. But it had been. He'd seen it. Held it. Victor banged the curved sink trap against the floor, cracking a tile down the center. He didn't care. He banged and banged again. He was angry. Angry and tired. Tired of losing things. Of having things taken from him.

Something slipped out the other end of the trap. Waterlogged and soft, it flopped out onto the tile floor amid the sluice of dirty drain water. Still. No movement. No cries.

Victor threw the sink trap aside and crawled to it. He scooped it up carefully, holding it in his hands. It was cold, slimy to the touch. He waited for it to make a noise. To cry out as it had before.

It was dead flesh, nothing more. If it had ever been anything else to begin with.

"I'm sorry," he said to it. It was a day for saying sorry.

And then, right there in his hands, it cried.

***

After he'd dried it carefully with a towel, Victor emerged from the bathroom with the ball of flesh cradled in his palms. He watched it breathe in his hands, so tiny and alive. Then he dug under the bed and found a shoebox Iris had left behind. He dumped out the shoes on the floor, found a heating blanket and laid it inside. He let the blanket get nice and warm before he laid the tiny ball in its new, heated bed.

The moment Victor let go, it began to cry again. This time it was louder, more urgent. A primal sound coming from a tiny mouth. The sound of it tugged at Victor's heart in a way he'd never felt before. He wanted only to protect this thing. It didn't matter what it was or where it had come from. Its life was in his hands. He was about to apologize when he realized it wouldn't help. No apologies would heal this.

"Please," he said, "please stop crying," but it only cried louder. He tried giving it food. He tried giving it milk. He thought about getting in his car and driving to the store for formula, but he didn't want to leave it alone, and he couldn't bring it with him, either. No one would understand.

"I don't know what you want," he said, nearly in tears himself. Was it in pain? Would he have to help the pain stop? He reached into the box, trying to tuck the blanket in better, figuring it might still be cold.

As he folded the blanket over, Victor's finger accidentally brushed against the thing's side. The moment it did, the crying stopped.

Only when he kept contact with it did it stop crying. It wouldn't take food. It wouldn't drink water. The only thing it asked for, the only thing it needed, was him.

Victor called out sick from work. He told them he was seeing someone about his cough.

***

The next day, everyone at work was being nicer to Victor than they had in a long time. They told him how happy they were he'd gone to see a doctor. "You're already sounding better," they said, and he agreed. He knew the real reason they were happy. They wouldn't have to listen to him cough anymore.

Victor sat at his desk and did his work. He caught up on what he'd missed from calling out. He was anxious, though. He could barely stay seated in his chair. Co-workers passed by his desk, pausing to tell him he was looking much better. The way his shirt was fitting him, he even looked like he was losing weight. He smiled and thanked them, letting them move on and get back to work. Finally, after about an hour, around the time he usually did, he left his desk and headed to the bathroom.

The bathrooms were private, one person at a time. Still acting casually, Victor stepped inside the men's room and locked the door behind him. He took a great big, breath, held it, then let it out. He really was doing much better. A few days earlier, taking in a breath like that would have ended quite differently.

Victor undid the buttons on his shirt and hung it carefully over the paper towel dispenser. Then he pulled his undershirt over his head and hung that up, too.

The square of gauze had held perfectly, secured firmly to the center of his chest with medical tape. He undid the top strip slowly, even though it hurt to go slow. He felt each hair ripping from his chest. He grimaced, but he didn't make a sound. No one could know what he was doing.

He knew the bandage had felt snug, tight beneath his shirt as he sat at his desk, but now he could see why. The ball of flesh was already bigger. It wasn't his imagination, it had nearly doubled in size since the beginning. It was starting to become defined as well. Vague arms and legs forming from its shapelessness. Above the fold it cried from, two small folds had appeared in the flesh.

"Look at you," he whispered, huddled over the sink.

The two new folds above its mouth parted. It looked up at him with beautiful, black eyes, tiny white pupils at the centers.

"Well, now you need a name," Victor said. He decided to call him Lungflower. Lungflower liked his name.

Victor brought Lungflower to work like this for a few days, but very quickly Lungflower grew too big to hide. There wasn't a shirt big enough in his closet that would do the trick. Lungflower could go a few minutes away from Victor's touch without screaming like it hurt him, but it wasn't enough, and Victor didn't feel right leaving him alone.

Victor came up with a hundred ideas how to sneak Lungflower into work. They were all insane or worse. Even if he could leave Lungflower at home, he didn't trust his neighbors. At least one of them had come snooping around the last time she heard crying, all because Victor tried to take a shower when

Lungflower was asleep. He made up a story about babysitting his nephew and left before any more questions could be asked.

He had one more idea. Victor called up his boss and asked if he could work from home, for medical reasons. There was nothing he did at work he couldn't do from home. But his boss said no. Nine years of loyalty meant nothing to them. Victor had no choice. He quit his job that day.

Lungflower had been in the world a week. He'd started the size of a plump cherry. Already he was the size of a baby. He held Victor's finger in his gray-pink hand and smiled up at him.

***

The early days at home with Lungflower were nice. Victor hadn't been without a job since the sixth grade. He'd always had so little time to himself. In fact he'd never had more than a few weeks vacation, and they were usually spent sitting on a beach or visiting Iris's family, neither of which held much appeal for him.

The new bedroom made a perfect nursery, Victor had been right about that. He bought as much sound-proofing material as he could get his hands on and lined the walls.

Lungflower didn't eat, though he sometimes looked hungry. He didn't drink, though he sometimes looked thirsty. Another week passed and Lungflower grew more and more. He was taller than a toddler and nearly twice as wide. He seemed to grow faster whenever he was hurt or scared, though that might have been Victor's imagination.

Checking that Lungflower was still asleep, Victor snuck out of the house early one morning to buy food for himself. The refrigerator was empty and so was his stomach. Before he could get into his car, he heard someone call out his name.

"Morning," Victor replied to his nosy neighbor.

"No more babysitting?" She asked him. "I haven't heard any crying lately."

Her eyes accused him. Victor didn't like that. He didn't like her. "Still babysitting," he said. "Just getting better at it."

When he came back from the store, Lungflower was awake. His screams were so loud they could be heard through the soundproofing. Victor threw the food down and ran to the nursery.

Lungflower had gotten bigger since Victor checked on him an hour earlier. Much bigger. He barely fit in his bed now, and his arms were as long as Victor's. Victor held him and told him he was sorry, that he'd never leave him. Not ever. He'd only gone out to get food.

It wasn't Victor's imagination. Lungflower grew faster when he was scared. He'd grown a strange fold at the center of his chest. Like a kangaroo's pouch.

***

Lungflower did eat something. Victor discovered it one evening by accident.

As the sun set through the kitchen window, Victor prepared himself dinner. He'd decided to make a meatloaf. He'd gotten good at cooking for himself over the past few weeks. His entire life, he'd always either lived with someone or had no reason to go through so much effort. Now he had a reason to take care of himself.

With Lungflower holding his leg, Victor gathered all his ingredients on the counter. Eggs, milk, bread crumbs, ketchup. He opened the package of chopped meat over the basin sink, draining off the excess blood before transferring it over to the large bowl on the center island.

Victor placed the chopped meat into the large bowl and began to add his other ingredients, kneading them together. The meat was cold, the ketchup colder, and his hands ached. Egg yolks burst between his fingers. Ketchup squished and mixed with the chopped meat. He glanced down to see how Lungflower was doing and found, to his surprise, that Lungflower wasn't by his side.

A moment of panic seized him. Lungflower never left his side. Never even let go of him. He prepared himself to search the house. To find something terrible. But the search didn't last long, and what he found wasn't terrible at all.

Lungflower was around the other side of the island, crouched over something he'd found. Victor hadn't noticed that when he'd transferred the meat from the sink to the island, a bit of it had slipped through his fingers and fallen to the floor. He watched as Lungflower's pinkish-gray hand reached out and claimed it. Brought the meat to his mouth. Before he could eat it, though, Lungflower turned and looked at Victor.

"It's okay," Victor said, smiling.

Lungflower ate raw meat. Victor tried to cook it, but when he did Lungflower spit it out. He tried to season it, marinate it, give it some kind of flavor.

Lungflower wouldn't take it. Victor began to buy more meat at the store. The more Lungflower ate, the more he could be on his own for small stretches of time. It gave him strength, and courage, and Victor wanted both for him.

When he thought about it, Victor realized he hadn't seen or heard a mouse in weeks.

Lungflower grew bigger than Victor. He grew bigger every day. He didn't speak, never tried to, but there was an intelligence behind his eyes that couldn't be ignored. And pain. Soon Lungflower barely fit under the doorways. Then he was hitting his head on the ceiling.

Victor bought more and more meat at the store. Whenever people started looking at him odd, he just went to a different store.

***

One night, well after he'd said goodnight to Lungflower in the living room, the only room Lungflower fit in anymore, and long after he'd drifted off to sleep, Victor woke up to the awful sound of Lungflower screaming.

He jumped from his bed and ran to check on him, to see what was causing him to make that terrible sound. His socks slipped on the worn-down wooden floor. He nearly knocked down a vase. When he reached the living room, he gasped at what he found.

Lungflower took up the entire living room. His thick neck was bent, head craned sideways against the ceiling. His black eyes looked at Victor, filled with so much pain. His massive legs were twisted like vines just to fit.

Victor had been worried about this moment. He'd been trying not to think of it, but it had arrived all the same. Lungflower simply couldn't fit in the house anymore. Not long ago, Lungflower couldn't stand to be apart from Victor. He'd cry if they weren't in contact. Flesh to flesh. Now it was Victor who was holding on. But doing so wasn't helping Lungflower. It was hurting him.

Stepping around the broken couch, Victor walked between Lungflower's tree-like legs. He went to Lungflower and laid his hand on his massive hand. The hand that had wrapped around Victor's finger once. Now each finger was as large as Victor's body.

"It's okay if you have to go," Victor said.

Lungflower's white pupils searched Victor. He cried out, the saddest sound Victor had ever heard. Lungflower sounded hungry. Hungry and scared.

"Listen to me. You're too big for this place. Too big and too strong. You don't belong here anymore. You've outgrown it."

Lungflower cried again, but he seemed to understand. He began to spread his arms and legs first. The walls moaned and cracked like old bones. Plaster cracked and wallpaper tore. A split opened in the ceiling, a lightning bolt of splinters. Dust fell like snow.

With enough room to breathe, Lungflower placed his gray-pink hands on the floor. His massive shoulders flexed and spread. It was better, but not enough. He looked once more at Victor.

Victor nodded. He went out the front door, walking backward all the way to the front yard. He watched as the house buckled and shook. Windows shattered outward. Shingles rained down on dead grass.

The roof opened like an egg hatching in the night. Like a flower in bloom, the house opened in front of Victor. The thing he had put all of his money into, all his time and passion.

Lungflower emerged from the remains of the crumbling house, born new into the night. Arms like redwoods stretched free. Black, wondrous eyes drank in the dark sky. It was a beautiful sight. The most beautiful Victor had ever seen.

He heard a voice intruding on the moment. His nosy neighbor was standing in her open doorway, dressed in a robe. In her hand was a phone. On her lips was panic. She was talking to the police, telling them to hurry, that something terrible was happening and that a man named Victor was to blame.

"It's not terrible," Victor called out to her as Lungflower slipped free of his prison.

"You stay away from me!" She screamed back. "You and whatever that thing is! I mean it!"

Lungflower didn't like that. He didn't like people yelling at Victor. The folds of his face shifted a way Victor had never seen them before. He'd seen Lungflower happy. He'd seen him scared and hungry, confused and content and even silly.

Victor had never seen him angry.

In three, massive strides, Lungflower went for the woman. With each step, Victor swore Lungflower grew another ten feet. The woman was frozen by the sight of it. She didn't try to run until the very last second. She ducked inside her house and slammed the door.

Lungflower turned to Victor, asking permission. Victor had watched from his cracked driveway. He was amazed to see Lungflower out in the world. When he shook his head, Lungflower reached out and grabbed Victor up from where he stood.

Lungflower could crush him like a cherry, a cherry with bones, but Victor wasn't afraid. He didn't fear dying, and he didn't have to. He knew Lungflower wouldn't hurt him. Lungflower might have grown a lot in the past few weeks, but he was still exactly the same. "You're doing so well," Victor told him. The vibrations of Lungflower's purring shook him. It felt good, like one of those massage chairs at the mall.

It wasn't long before the police showed up. Lungflower was scared of all the cars at his feet, their flashing lights and sirens. Victor told him to stay calm. The two of them ignored the noise and the lights for a while, ignored the men trying to speak to them through bullhorns. Victor pointed out all the new sights and told Lungflower what they were called. Lungflower liked the telephone wires best.

"Stay calm, Victor," one of the police said through his bullhorn. "We called your wife. She's on her way."

"I don't have a wife," Victor replied. He glanced at the house they'd once shared. It was nothing more than a pile of sticks and moldy insulation. A cheap gazebo in the backyard. Maybe that was all it had ever been. Victor looked up at Lungflower, the way Lungflower had once looked up at him. "There's nothing here for us," he said.

Lungflower's black eyes understood. He slipped Victor into the fold in his chest. Like a kangaroo's pouch. Then he ran, leaving the shouting police and the pile of sticks behind.

***

Lungflower's footsteps shook the earth. The streets trembled and cracked under his feet. People screamed and cried and prayed and took their pictures. And all the while, Lungflower grew bigger.

Victor watched from the warmth of Lungflower's chest as houses fell. He smiled as office buildings broke and electrical boxes exploded. Power lines and telephone wires- Lungflower's favorite- snapped under his feet like overused fishing line. And still he grew bigger. And bigger. Because even though he was massive, even though things crumbled and burned with each move he made, he still felt everything.

Everything he broke hurt him, too. Everything he ruined, ruined him back.

Soon the men with guns came. They fired at Lungflower, scaring him, leaving black marks across his skin. But no matter how much they threw at him, how many bullets they fired and explosives they launched, Lungflower didn't fight back. He only protected Victor. Shielded him from the pain.

Bigger and bigger Lungflower grew. Bigger and bigger the guns came. As fire lit up the sky, reflecting like bright orange petals in Lungflower's eyes, Victor realized a terrible truth: Lungflower had one downfall, one weakness in this world.

Him.

Victor had been all that Lungflower had needed in the beginning, but now, out in the world, Victor was holding him back. A crutch. A heated blanket.

Down in the crowd of flashing lights and violent men far below, behind the orange and white barricades, Victor saw a face he'd known in another life. They'd shared a house once. A future. He didn't resent her in the slightest. Not anymore. He was grateful to her. He was happy she was here to see this.

Without hesitation, Victor jumped. He threw himself free before Lungflower could stop him. He fell like a raindrop, down, down, down Lungflower's incredible height, soft wind in his hair, his clothes flapping like a flag. All the way down, his eyes filled up with tears as he beheld how big Lungflower had grown. He was so happy, he barely felt the impact.

***

As he lay on the ground, blood pooling around him, filling up the cracks in the dirt to water the earth, Lungflower bent down, down, down to see him, to bring his vast face close to Victor's. Even then, somewhere in the distance of faded sound, the guns still fired.

"They're scared," Victor told him. "They're scared because you're strong." Victor's eyes began to go dark. Shadows closed in like a warm blanket. He looked into Lungflower's eye, at the sadness there. The pain. But even then he knew what else was behind it. "Are you hungry?" He asked.

Lungflower simply nodded. Victor smiled up at him, the way Lungflower had once smiled up at Victor.

"It's okay, son," he said. "It's okay."

The word was all he needed. Lungflower rose. He turned to the people firing at him, turned to consume them all. His capacity to love was endless, but all those people would never know that. They would only know his other, unending side. His hunger. As Victor's eyes went black, he felt his chest swell with pride. Pride and something else.

When Lungflower had grown in his lungs, back in what felt like a lifetime ago, Victor had developed a cough. A nagging, painful cough, like thistles deep down. But Victor understood it now. The coughing wasn't because he was sick, it was because he'd tried to keep it in. To deny what was happening. To hold back the beauty of the change.

This time he'd denied nothing. Held back nothing. This time he'd been ready for the beauty. Ready for the transformation.

The truth was, Victor had felt it for days. A thousand seeds sprouting inside.

***

The Body Farm

1.

I feel the need to explain myself. I'm not a guy who gets scared easily, but I'm also not the kind who keeps his head in the sand, if you know what I mean. When something doesn't feel right, it just doesn't feel right, period. I acknowledge that most of the bad things that happen in life can be blamed on people or the world around us, but I also believe there are things that fall outside those two categories, at least until we prove otherwise.

Like what happened at the body farm.

I've wanted to be a writer ever since I was a kid, so forgive me if I get too flowery sometimes, it's the habits of a writer. As I'm sure you know, though, writing doesn't pay the bills, and despite my dream of earning a living by writing, I've always needed a day job to get me by. Through the father of a friend, I ended up getting trained and certified as an unarmed security guard straight out of high school, which I did all the way through college. It was easy, and the money was good enough for a while, but eventually I looked for something with a future in it. So long as my writing wasn't taking off, I figured I might as well build a career. After a long search I got a job at one of the major banks- which one I'd rather not say.

Six years I spent working my ass off, climbing my way up the ranks. That was until five weeks ago when they decided they had too many branches open on the east coast, as well as too many employees working those branches. So I got the boot. No severance, no fanfare, no apology, I was out on the street, and as I soon found out, no one was hiring.

When things started to get desperate I paid a visit to this employment agency up the block from my house. I've never liked the guy who runs it, but as I said, times are desperate. So I walked in and signed up. They didn't seem too hopeful when I asked about other bank jobs, but when they saw the security guard experience on my resume' they perked up. As it turned out they had an overnight temp guard position they were having trouble filling. Needless to say I was hesitant to take what I believed was a step backward. Not to down-talk or discredit guard work in any way, it just doesn't fit the direction I'm trying to go in at the moment. You'd think being an overnight guard would afford me plenty of time to write, but the truth is I've always had a hard time writing while completely alone. For some reason it makes me uneasy, and I end up getting nothing done.

The point is, I didn't want to take the gig, but a man's gotta eat. My choice was helped by the rate they were paying, which was at the higher end of what guards usually make. Against my better judgment I accepted. They made a few phone calls, wrote down an address and sent me on my way. "It's on the water," is the only detail they gave. My old uniform was a bit snug but it still fit. I actually found that fact a little disappointing.

Around five o'clock I arrived at the address they'd written on the card, which it turned out was a boat launch to get over to an island, on which was the actual gig. I'll call it Twain Island, since I'm pretty sure I'm not supposed to be talking about it in the first place, even though its actual name is one I'd never heard despite growing up close-by. After a confusing exchange with the older guy who ran the dock, he told me something which very nearly made me turn around and get back in my car.

"I need to see your phone," he said. I was confused, but I took it out of my pocket and showed him. Then he said, "If that's a camera, I need to take it." I made a joke, something like, "What's on that island, the Queen of England?" but he wasn't amused. I argued with him for a minute but in the end I handed it over. Like I said, a man's gotta eat. A few minutes later an even older guy came got me and took me onto the boat. Since it was only the two of us, and since I had no idea what I had gotten myself into, I tried to make some small-talk. The guy wasn't very talkative, but as we approached the island he made the second sketchy comment of the day, this one in the form of a question.

"Have you ever been to one of these farms?" I told him I'd been to plenty of farms, to which he said, "Not like this one you haven't." I had no idea what he was talking about, but by then we were already pulling up to the dock that stuck out from the rocky shore. We docked. Before I could ask where I was supposed to go he was already pulling away. It seemed he didn't want to stick around long. There was a building up the way's a bit which looked like an old rec center. Given that I had nowhere else to go, I headed for the building. Halfway across the lawn was a sign which read, "[Twain] Island Forensic Anthropology Facility." They were words I was familiar with separately, but together lost their meaning. As I contemplated exactly what they meant, a young guy wearing a guard's uniform came around the side of the building and waved me down.

"I heard the boat," he said. He introduced himself as Eric and handed me a walkie-talkie. He explained that, other than a few computers with an internet connection, all communication on the island was done by old-school means. In case of emergency they even had a two-way radio set-up. I asked him why I wasn't allowed to bring my cell and he said it was so no pictures ended up on the internet, which I'd heard from a friend who did guard work at a high-end jewelry manufacturer, so it made some sense. It still didn't tell me what the hell was going on out on that island.

I point-blank asked him. All he said was, "C'mon, I'll show you."

We walked not into but around the decent-sized building, past a second, smaller building and into the woods beyond. Eric said something about the island being the alleged site of buried pirate treasure, but to be honest I wasn't paying much attention at that point. There was a strong smell in the air, pungent and sweet and downright awful which I found impossible to ignore. Eric noticed my face and said, "Ever smell a dead body before?" I shook my head no. He said, "You'll never forget it now."

At that point we came into a clearing in the woods where the foul odor really ramped up. I've always had a strong stomach, but even this was excessive. I felt a ball form at the back of my throat. There were two people, one male, one female, both roughly college-aged and wearing similar, gray coats standing over what looked like long, low cages made of chicken wire. As we walked closer I could see dark forms in the cages like piles of trash. The girl looked over at us and nodded politely but the guy didn't bother. She was pretty and he looked like a bug. It wasn't until we were right on top of the cages that I realized what they held.

The first body I saw, in fact have ever seen, was a woman's. Her skin was impossibly waxy with large patches of discoloration, as if the wax had been burned. She looked like someone had sprinkled rice across her, like a new bride. Unfortunately, it wasn't rice. The maggots crawled on her legs and pooled in the crevices of her neck. Her surprisingly white teeth grinned up at me, exposed, and her belly was inflated like a birthday balloon. My mouth watered from the rising feel of vomit but I managed to keep it in check. It helped to not look at her creeping skin.

He introduced the two as Bernard and Terri, interns from the [name removed] Institute, and said there were two more wandering around somewhere, as well as the man in charge, a scientist by the name of Doctor Christianson. Terri could see I was bothered, so she was nice enough to finally explain what was going on. "We study human decomposition," she said. The goal was to better understand the process in order to help, among other things, police determine more accurate times of death in a variety of settings.

I looked at the five or six other cages, which she explained were to keep birds away, and asked how many there were on the island. "It varies," she said, "but it usually hovers somewhere around fifty."

Fifty dead bodies. One island. No boats.

They said some see-you-laters and then Eric led me around the rest of the island, first to point out some of the other body sites- more corpses, some caged, some not- and then to perform a perimeter around the shore. He said I'd have to do at least two such rounds during my shift, which I was already thinking about skipping. It took about forty-five minutes for us to circle back around to the dock, which I noticed was the only way onto or off of the island short of risking the waves crashing onto the sharp rocks and the ring of slimy garbage. By then the sun was starting to set. Then he took me inside the main research building which as I'd guessed had been converted from a sports center dating back some fifty years. We took a quick look around at the operation and I saw the back of someone's head inside one of the rooms, but other than that not much registered. I think by that time my head was spinning too fast for any more information to get in.

We left the main building and went to the second building which served as the guard's office. Eric pointed out the bathroom, the lockers, the eating area with stocked fridge, the flashlights, the desk with the two-way radio, which he showed me how to use, though by then he was eyeing his watch. He gave me a grin and asked if I was all set. I shrugged, which was the most sincere answer I could give.

"I'll be honest," he told me, "most guys don't last long here. Especially the night-shifters."

"Thanks."

"If you take out the mental part it's the easiest job in the world. But that mental part..." His voice trailed off, and I knew exactly what he meant. What could be easier than making sure a bunch of stiffs stayed dead? And yet with the sun going down I was filled completely with dread, the kind where you want to run and scream in no particular direction. Before I could articulate the thought, the sound of a docking boat rose up, and with a nod and a few more last-minute instructions about filling out the log book, he was gone.

"Next boat's at three a.m.," he shouted from across the lawn, which seemed like a pretty important detail to be leaving for the last second. Ahead of him were the two interns I'd met, Bernard and Terri, along with two others. Terri waved and I waved back, pretending to be unfazed. On the boat already, aside from the old man operating it, was a man whose face I couldn't make out from a distance other than a beard. I assumed it was Doctor Christianson, though I had no way of knowing for sure.

After the boat chugged away and made a line for land, I looked around at the dimming island, inhabited by me and fifty rotting corpses, give or take, with the wind kicking up off the ocean, and wondered how I'd ended up that way. Just a month earlier I'd been sitting comfortably behind a desk in a warm bank. It was incredible how quickly life could shift beneath your feet.

I retreated back inside the guard's office and immediately decided to stay in it until the boat came to get me at three. I locked the door. Screw the promises, screw the temp agency, screw the Twain Island Forensic Anthropology Facility, I wasn't about to go stumbling around in the dark on an island full of dead people, caged or otherwise. There was no way anyone would know one way or the other whether I'd done my rounds or not, and I had a hard time believing that anyone would want to get onto the island, let alone be able to pull up to the dock and get past me without being heard.

To pass the time I had the internet, thankfully, and that got me past the first few mindless hours. Before I knew it the clock over the door read twenty past nine o'clock. Outside it was pitch black, while inside it was way too quiet, so I pulled up some music videos and let them play in the background, a huge playlist of classic rock songs, as I opened a text file and thought of some story ideas I'd like to explore. Not surprisingly, most of them had to do with zombies coming to life and attacking the living. Nothing really stuck, though, and I began to have that familiar uneasy feeling that comes whenever I try to write alone. After a few minutes I stopped trying to fight it. I closed the file and then my eyes.

I'm not sure how long I was asleep. What I do know is what woke me up. With my eyes still closed I started to become aware of a sound under the music, the playlist still coming out of the computer's speaker, which was faint but getting louder. It was far off in the island, but I could make it out as clear as anything.

And I know it sounds crazy. I really know it does. But it was a woman crying.

When I realized this, my eyes shot open. I jumped out of the chair, grabbed my walkie-talkie and flashlight and ran out of the office, turning on the flashlight as I came around the building. I stopped for a second and shone the light into the forest, catching nothing but the trunks and leaves. For a second I wondered if I'd actually heard the cries or if I'd been half in a dream, the way light sleep messes with you, but then I heard a shout, definitely a woman's pitch, and I bolted into the woods. All I could think was some idiot had found their way onto the island, maybe even a group of idiots, thrill-seeking kids, and hurt themselves on my watch. I would have to carefully forge the log book to cover my ass on this one.

That already familiar stench came to my nose as I came into the first clearing. My flashlight picked up the metal of the cages. I stopped running. I remembered myself, where I was and why I had locked myself in the office. Those cages, just sitting there in the dark. Corpses staring up. Maggots and flies. The cries had stopped, which had me thinking either I was being pranked or much worse: I was too late to help whoever it had been.

I did what I swore I wouldn't, which was the job they'd hired me to do. With a major amount of hesitation I did my rounds. Either I would find the woman, I figured, or I could honestly tell the Doctor that I'd secured the island when they found a body in the morning. Another body, that is. A new one. As I walked the edge of the island I formed a joke in my head about how they could leave the dead woman where they found her and just add her to the guest list. The joke always ended with me saying, "You're welcome."

I'll be honest, I didn't do a full perimeter, but I did do most of one. Other than half of a hollowed out horseshoe crab I didn't find anything, so I cut back toward the first clearing where I'd sworn the woman's cries had came from. I walked slowly in case I came across any more body sites, especially the uncaged kind, which I didn't want to stumble over in the dark despite the little yellow flags that marked them. The smell would probably warn me first, except for the really long-gone ones, the piles of bones which still stunk but not nearly as much. Needless to say, I was relieved when I reached the clearing.

The beam of my flashlight caught the top of the cages as I walked between them, using them as a guide back to the office without really focusing on them. For some reason I still don't understand, maybe because my eyes picked up something different in the dark, or maybe I felt a change in the air, I shone the light into the last cage, the first I'd seen a few hours earlier, where the bloated woman had grinned up at me.

My feet stopped. So did my heart. What my flashlight saw, what I saw, changed me forever. And I know it sounds crazy. I really know it does. But the cage was empty.

I got in closer to get a better look, because there was no way what I was seeing was real, but I was horrified to find it was. The body was gone, the only thing left of it a long patch of dead grass, a puddle of half-dried fluids, and strips of what looked like leather but I knew wasn't leather. The cage around it was left exactly where I'd seen it. Only the body had disappeared.

As I stared down at the empty cage, my walkie-talkie crackled in my pocket. It made me jump a bit, the sudden noise in the night, and I fished it out of my pocket where I'd forgotten I put it during the perimeter sweep. But if the first sound made me jump, the second made my skin crawl worse than one of the corpses behind me.

A woman was whispering on the other end. I turned the volume up and pressed the speaker to my ear to hear better. The words were too low to make out, only the distinctly female tone, the same as the one who had called out from somewhere in the woods. Nervous, I brought the walkie-talkie to my mouth and pressed the button on the side.

"Hello? Who's there?" I tried to sound like I was in charge but it wasn't convincing. I let go of the button and brought the speaker back to my ear, straining to hear the whispers.

A laugh. A woman's laugh, high-pitched and delirious, came through the speaker.

Instinct took over and I ran. I ran away from the cages and out of the clearing, into the woods and out of them again until I was running between the two buildings and back into the office, slammed the door shut and locked it. My pulse throbbed in my neck and I tried to catch myself with my hands on the desk, taking great, big breaths of air in.

Breaths of air. Stale air. Not just stale, but wretched. Sickly sweet and pungent, the smell of those bodies had somehow moved into the guard's office, even though none of the sites were anywhere near it, even with a strong wind to push the air around the island.

It was then, as I pushed myself up off the desk, that I thought again of the missing body. The woman's body. The woman's voice on the radio, the whispers and the laugh. It was then that I realized not just the air had gotten into the building.

I looked at my hand- a smudge of something black was on my palm. There was a matching one on the table.

2

They asked me to go back.

It was three days ago I was picked up tired and hungry on that dock. The captain had found me with a dying flashlight in one hand and a turned-off radio in the other. This time I was the one who didn't say much, I just got out of the boat, drove home in a daze and fell asleep in my bed. I spent a lot of the time since thinking about what I'd experienced on Twain Island, the rest of it applying to jobs who didn't call back. I went back and read what I wrote. It sounds almost ridiculous now, like the ravings of a wild man, especially happening so soon after I woke up. The more I thought about it, the less real it seemed.

As I was applying for other guard jobs, the guy who runs the temp agency called me to tell me the Forensic Anthropology Facility had contacted them to ask about hiring me again. With no hesitation I told him I had no interest in going back to that island. While I was at it, I thanked him for not warning me about the nature of their research. He swore to me he didn't know- I didn't believe him- and told me before I made up my mind that they were willing to raise their rate by almost thirty percent. "I think they're tired of giving the free tour, if you know what I mean," he said.

It's hard to argue with that kind of money when you're unemployed. There was still the whole matter of the disappearing body, and the creepy laughter, and the traces of death in the guard's office, which were three very good reasons to never go back. I couldn't exactly ask him about all that without sounding insane, so I asked him the next best thing. "Did they have any complaints about the last time," I asked. The way I figured, if a body got up and walked away on my watch, they might think I had something to do with it.

"If they had any complaints," he said, "I doubt we'd be talking right now."

He was right, of course. The whole thing was feeling more and more like something I'd dreamed up. About an hour earlier I had checked my bank account, which was getting grim, and now here I was saying no to a cushy paycheck. I thought of Eric's advice, how it was the easiest job in the world so long as you could manage the mental bit. Then I thought of my dad who worked in high-rise construction for thirty years, and once drove himself back to a job site after having his thumb sewn back on so he could finish out the day.

God help me, I went.

A thought occurred to me as the boat captain drove me over to the island: what if the body actually had gone missing and they were luring me back to question me about it, or even catch me in the act of doing it again? What if they'd gone to the cops but didn't have enough evidence to accuse me? My stomach sank, and I looked over at the old guy at the wheel. He looked back at me with a funny look in his eye. Maybe it was something. Maybe it was nothing. It was too late to turn around now.

When I got to the island it was still bright out, which helped get me off the dock and onto land, and I was interested to notice that no one had come to greet me when I arrived. I took it as a good sign and went to track down Eric. It didn't take long- he was at the computer in the guard's office.

"I didn't think I'd see you around here again," he said with a laugh. Apparently the boat captain told everyone how ready I was to leave when he pulled up the other day. It was a little embarrassing, but to be fair no one had prepared me for the kind of shit I'd shown up for. Eric found it hilarious but I could tell he understood where I was coming from. While we were on the subject, I asked him if he had ever heard anything weird on the island, especially on the night shift. He asked me what kind of weird. "I don't know. Stuff moving. Voices."

He got a soda from the fridge. "Uh oh. Don't tell me you're the superstitious type. That doesn't really fly here." As he chugged the soda down I assured him I was a rational person, but he seemed skeptical. According to him, despite Twain Island being an island, there were still plenty of animals that lived there. Some swam over, others came over on boats or floating garbage. "We've asked Doctor Christianson about animal control but he says it would ruin the balance of nature, which is important for their data or whatever. I think he just doesn't want to pay for it out of his grant money."

It wasn't the first time I got the vibe no one liked the doctor. After I finished catching up with Eric he threw away his empty can and announced he was going to complete his final rounds before it was time to go home. I think he expected me to hang out in the office, like he would if he could, so it surprised him when I headed out in the opposite direction. I wanted to reacquaint myself with the island and the interns. Based on the look he gave me, he definitely thought I was a crazy person.

The real reason for my walk was even crazier than he suspected.

No one was working in the main clearing, so I used the privacy to check the cage where the body had disappeared, or where I'd convinced myself it had, at this point I didn't know what to think. It had been an uneventful return so far and I doubted I would get such a mild reception if they suspected me of something as gross as grave robbing.

So as you can imagine, I was especially confused when I found the woman inside the cage. There like she never left. She was less an inflated bag of maggots by now, more skin and bones than the last time I'd seen her. Her rotting body was oddly comforting.

When I turned away from her, Bernard the intern was standing at the other side of the clearing with a clipboard in one hand and a ruler in the other, checking on one of the other bodies. I don't know how long he'd been there but when I turned to leave he threw me a look too nasty to ignore. Instead of heading back to the office as planned I went his way and struck up a conversation. Something pointless about the weather which he stayed quiet through. When I was done with my bit, he not-so-subtly changed the subject.

He asked me what my interest was in the female specimen, and the way he asked it I understood what he was implying, which by the way is disgusting. I didn't know how to answer him without sounding insane, so I told him I'd heard some sounds out this way the last time, but when I came to inspect the site there was nobody there. But what he said next made my legs go cold.

"Did you move her?"

It took me a second. I said no, no, I definitely didn't, and would have no reason to, and I asked him why he would ask something like that. He didn't want to say at first, but after I asked a few times he told me the photos hadn't matched up from one day to the next. Specifically the position of the body.

I asked him if it was possibly animals, the ones Eric told me lived on the island, the garbage-riders. Like I was a child who'd asked a dumb question in class, he tapped the cage next to him with his foot and looked at me to say, "that's what these are for." "What about gases," I asked, all those things that happen when we decompose, couldn't that move a body? With no lack of attitude he assured me he knew which movements were natural and which ones weren't. "She was definitely moved. If it was you, you're better off coming clean." I could see he wasn't going to bend on this, so I told him it wasn't me, and if he didn't believe me it wasn't my problem, and I went back to the guard's office. But I'd be lying if I said our conversation didn't weigh on me for a long time after that.

By the time Eric got back from his final rounds I was in a dark place. My thoughts were spiraling down and I was angry at myself for coming back to the island. I was giving strong thought to quitting and hitching a ride back on the late boat, and Eric could probably tell, since he was acting especially light and jokey, trying to improve the mood in the guard's office. I suspected it was less for me and more for himself, which he proved when he casually dropped that he had some big plans for the night, which would have been ruined if I hadn't shown up.

At that point Terri popped her head in for a few minutes to say hi and ask Eric a question about the alarm system in the main research building. Before she left she told me it was good to see me again. After she was gone Eric chuckled and said how obvious it was that Terri was into me. I told him that was bullshit. "Why do you think they asked you back," he asked.

"You were tired of giving the free tour," I quoted.

"There's other guys they could have asked. And she brought your name up like five times in the past three days. Said you have 'kind eyes.' Who else were they gonna bring back?"

I didn't put much faith in what Eric said, but it beat thinking about other things. It didn't hurt that Terri was pretty cute- in a weird, works-with-dead-bodies way. The thought of asking her out distracted me for a while. Soon enough I was alone. The boat came and left and like an idiot I didn't get on it.

I spent the first hour like the first night, on the internet, visiting the usual time-wasters, but after a while I started to think about what Bernard had said. To be honest, it pissed me off. This guy, this bug-looking prick, doesn't even know me, wasn't even there that night, yet he thinks he can throw around disgusting accusations. Pretty soon I wasn't paying attention to the screen- I was thinking about cornering Bernard in one of the more private areas of the woods and giving him something real to accuse me of. I'm not an outwardly violent guy, but that doesn't mean I'm incapable of it.

Something by the door caught my attention. Movement. I turned in time to catch a spot of darkness moving past the window, and for the second time that day my legs went cold.

The shadow was in the vague shape of a person. I'd like to say that I jumped out of my chair, flung the door open and jumped on the intruder like a damn security guard, but the truth is I stayed as still as I could. I listened to the grass rustle and I didn't move a muscle until the sound was gone. A minute later I stood at the open door, shining my flashlight into the dark. And even though I didn't want to, even though I hated to admit it, I found myself surrounded by the very familiar, very strong smell of rotting corpse.

My first instinct was to step back inside and lock the door, radio the police and shut myself in a broom closet until help arrived. But I also knew that dead bodies don't get up and walk around, that those things don't happen except in movies. I pictured my dad and what he would do in this situation if he was still alive. He would find whoever was screwing with him and jam his reattached thumb into their eye.

My attached one would have to do.

Due to an overcast night, the woods were already black. The way the flashlight's beam pierced the night reminded me of footage of deep-sea divers. I moved quietly between the trees and toward the main clearing and strained to hear even the slightest sound of footsteps or movement in the woods ahead of or around me, but other than the wind and the ocean I couldn't hear a thing. What made me happiest, though, was finding the woman's body in its cage where it belonged- even now that sounds like an unbelievable thing to find relief in- and after a quick check I discovered all of her roommates were in their respective cages, too, at least in this site. Taking courage from that, I decided to finally do some proper rounds.

There was a mystery on that island, something the employees weren't telling me, and it was time I figured it out.

I moved into the woods at a sharp angle, aiming to reach the shore at a particular spot I'd seen with Eric the other day, a point at the island's highest where he said you could see a small cave opening at low tide. The point itself didn't matter so long as I had a target, though something about the overcast night got me confused, not being able to use the moon or stars as reference, and after a couple of minutes I found myself turned around. As it turns out, the island is larger than I'd thought at first, and it's very possible to get lost on it. I tried to correct my path using the sound of the ocean- just keep heading toward the waves- but after a minute I came into a clearing and was surprised to find it was the one I had left a few minutes earlier.

If I were a smarter man I would have said screw it and returned to the office, but my decision to find answers had made me too stubborn to take the easy way out. Instead I turned around and headed once again for the same spot on the shore. This time I made an even sharper angle. There was no way I was going to end up back in that clearing.

The good news is, I didn't. The bad news is I became completely disoriented by the night and the tree after tree after identical tree, and it wasn't long before I couldn't even tell which way the ocean was, the sound of waves coming through from all directions. Twice I came across body cages but I didn't stop long enough to get a look at them. It was bad enough putting my back to them in the dark. Thinking about their dead eyes on me put some speed in my step. If you've ever been lost, you know the feeling of frustration and hopelessness it brings, how you kick yourself for being so stupid. You blame yourself for every mistake you've ever made. Whether or not you believe in God, you start making pacts and promises. "If you just get me out of this, I promise to be a better person," even though you fully intend to forget everything you said the moment you're found again. Bottle up that feeling and let it loose on an island of cadavers, and you'll start to understand what went through my head in those woods.

When I got really desperate, I started to notice the smell of rotting meat.

With the breeze blowing so erratically through the trees I couldn't get a bearing on which direction the stink came from. Whether it was following me or I was following it wasn't clear. Only one thing was: it was getting stronger. I didn't know if I should walk slower to keep from stepping in something or run away from someone pursuing me. As much as I wanted to check the trees, my flashlight stayed trained on the ground, and thank God it did. Out of nowhere I came across a body, a pair of purple feet sticking up from a patch of green ivy. It wasn't even marked with a flag, which I thought was extremely dangerous, and if it had been, the flag had fallen and disappeared under the thick vines. The body was muscular, definitely a man, and as I got closer I saw it was missing its head and one of its arms. Flies buzzed on its freshly ruptured skin. Their whining voices got under my own skin, into my eardrums, and nausea bubbled up in my stomach, the taste of acid at the back of my throat.

I threw up behind a tree. Doubled over, wiping my mouth clean, a stick snapped somewhere in the woods under weight, as if someone had stepped on it.

I straightened up and aimed my flashlight toward the sound of approaching footsteps, and I called out, "Who's there?" The beam of light found feet, not the corpse's feet but walking feet, feet wearing shoes, feet attached to legs and pants and a gray coat.

"You're contaminating my site," the bearded man said. I didn't have to ask him for identification- it was Doctor Christianson. "The other guards don't come this far inland."

"To be honest I'm a little lost," I admitted to him.

"This isn't the place to do that," he said as he walked over. I agreed completely. I told him I thought everyone had gone home by now. "I'm one of those fortunate few who does what he loves," he said. "I get lost in the work."

I wasn't sure how the statement made me feel about the doctor. On the one hand I admired his work ethic, but on the other a man who can get lost in this kind of work doesn't exactly make you feel comfortable being around him at night. "You missed the boat," I told him, but he shrugged it off. "If I call for another, another comes," he explained.

"Did you happen to walk past the guard's office a little while ago?"

His face shifted. "Are you keeping track of me?" I shook my head no. "You worry about people trying to get onto the island. I'll worry about what they do while they're here."

I nodded. There wasn't any arguing with a prick like that. He pointed me in the right direction back to the buildings. I thanked him and went to leave, but at the last second I turned back. There was something I needed to know. "This really doesn't bother you," I asked, but his expression told me everything. He was tired of this question, and not just tired of it, above it.

"I find it fascinating, not that I need to. The data I gather here will give police the evidence they need to catch countless criminals."

"I guess I can't get over the fact that they used to be people. That guy right there," I pointed, "do you even know his name?"

The doctor no longer looked like he wanted to humor me. "By any remote chance, do you know why I asked you back," he asked. I told him probably because everyone else said no. "Because I don't like to answer questions. That's why I chose an island for my research in the first place."

"They say no man is an island," I offered, because I couldn't think of what else to say.

"'They' are worried about being popular."

That certainly wasn't a problem he shared. I thanked him for helping me find my way, but by that time he wasn't paying attention to me anymore, he was studying the headless man and taking down some notes, so I left without another word and headed in the direction he'd said. It was surprisingly easy to find my way back after that. Within twenty minutes I was standing in front of the open door of the guard's office. As I entered the building, I tried to remember for the life of me if I'd left the door open. I tell you, I could have sworn I closed it.

I took a quick piss in the cramped bathroom, washed my hands and grabbed a soda from the fridge, downing it in three, long swigs. I threw the can in the garbage pail where it joined Eric's and a few others. It seemed they were more concerned with recycling people than they were aluminum.

There was a big cork-board hung up in the eating area with a bunch of random things tacked to it- health notices, old flyers, a few articles cut out of medical magazines- but it was the photo that caught my attention. It was one of those unflattering pictures people love to take of each other at work. Messy hair and a few extra pounds only matter if it's a picture of you, right? It seemed like a recent photo, probably taken with one of the digital cameras they use to photograph the bodies and printed out on the office printer, yet I didn't recognize the guy in it. He was in fairly good shape, arms bulged against the short sleeves of his guard's uniform. On his right forearm he had a tattoo of a green snake wrapped around a red apple.

I thought back to the body in the middle of the woods, where Doctor Christianson and I had talked. No cage, no flag, pretty muscular, missing the head as well as one of the arms.

Missing an arm. The right arm.

Just to be safe, I locked the door.

3.

You'd think I was crazy if I said I went back to Twain Island for even one more night. It's okay to admit it, you'd be right. But I have to admit something, too: I suffer from a case of curiosity. I can't help but stick my nose in strange business. Maybe that's what appealed to me about guard work in the first place, the idea of seeking out trouble. It seems like all those hours behind a desk weren't able to wipe it out.

It also helped that they asked me to cover a day shift this time- Eric called out sick- which seemed to me way safer than another graveyard shift. Maybe it's childish to feel that way, like I'm a little kid who's scared of the dark, but at least in the daytime I can see what's coming at me. Not to mention I wouldn't be alone on the island during the day. I might even get some answers about what was going on out there if I spied around, talked to the right people, asked the right questions.

Just to be clear, though, I did ask the employment agency if there were other gigs. Any other gigs. You can see where this is going.

Maybe it was the warm sun and knowing I'd be off the island before it went away, or maybe it was the pocket knife in my back pocket, but when I handed my cell phone over to the guy who ran the dock I was feeling a bit bold. I asked him if there were any interesting local stories about Twain Island. At first he shrugged it off and said, "Every place has its stories," but then he said there was one thing, a story he'd heard more than once, from more than one neighbor, which might be of interest. He said strange lights had been seen on the island, either from the shore or by passing boats. To say the story was disappointing would be an understatement. I told him it was most likely just the flashlights of guards doing their rounds.

He nodded and said, "You're probably right." As I was leaving I heard him mumble, "Pretty stupid to use red flashlights."

Out on the dock, Terri, Bernard and another assistant were by the boat waiting for me to arrive. The captain was on the boat reading a magazine. When he saw me he put it down and started the engine. Terri smiled and said hi, as did the other assistant, a heavier guy named Miguel. As always Bernard was a creep and said nothing. That was until we got out on open water and Terri started making some small talk.

"So you can't stay away, huh," she asked.

"What can I say? Apparently I need this money stuff to live."

She laughed. I was feeling pretty good about myself, until Bernard chimed in. "That's not all you get out of it," he said. I couldn't stand this guy any longer. I leaned past Terri and asked him what his problem was. "Night-shifters," he said.

"Look around," I told him. "I'm working a day shift."

"You're still a night-shifter." He didn't even want to look me in the eye. I wanted to punch him in his, but Terri got involved and asked what was bothering him. He started spouting some bullshit about fetishes and fascinations with death and all this stuff that he knew a little too much about. Miguel just shook his head and laughed at what Bernard was saying, but Terri to her credit did her best to defuse the little creep. By the time we docked he was calmer but still not looking my way, which was fine by me. Before he walked off he turned back to me and said, "Do whatever you want to the bodies. Just stay away from me."

Terri must have seen that I was about to pounce on him. She got in front of me and pulled me in the other direction, saying she needed some help carrying some heavy boxes. She was clearly appealing to my ego. I decided to drop it. The little idiot wasn't about to ruin my chances with a cute girl. That would be letting him win.

As we walked to the main research building I realized Doctor Christianson hadn't come over with us. Terri explained that he usually comes over alone, whenever he decides to start his day, and her saying that reminded me of the conversation I had with him the other night about missing the last boat. "If I call for another, another comes," he'd said. Terri laughed and said it sounded like something an egomaniac like him would say. I was digging her more and more by the minute. We entered the research building and continued down the hall.

"Sorry about Bernard," she said. "Forensics attracts the occasional weirdo."

"Is that what brought you to it," I joked.

"Actually it was because my brother died."

"Oh. Shit." I felt my face go red at my bad joke.

"It's fine," she waved it off. "We were really close. He donated his body to science and it ended up in a facility like this one. When I looked into forensic anthropology I was hooked. I went right to the university and changed my major. I know it sounds funny but I feel close to him here."

It did sound weird, but I'd heard of worse ways for coping with grief. When my dad died I spent the first month so drunk I can barely remember it except for what people tell me. I even spent a night in jail for breaking a bartender's nose, though that's a story for another time. Terri and I went through a door at the end of hall where the sign simply read: "Cleaning."

The room was about the size of a small kitchen and had all kinds of tools and chemicals for cleaning skeletons once they had served their purpose on the farm. Terri showed me the whole operation, explaining that after being cleaned here the bones went to another room for storage or shipping, depending on their final home. "But you don't need to go in there," she said, "it's just a bunch of bones."

"What was the name of the overnight guard who worked before me," I asked out of the blue. She seemed caught by surprise, but she thought for a second and said his name was Greg. "Is he the guy with the tattoo?" I pointed to my forearm.

"Yeah. How'd you know?" I told her there was a picture of him hanging in the guard's office. She nodded, remembering the picture. "It's too bad he left." I asked her why and she said, "Well...he was kind of cute."

At that point the door opened and Doctor Christianson appeared in the doorway. He seemed annoyed by my being there. "I think you'll find no one in here needs guarding," he said, then glanced at Terri. Terri apologized and explained she needed my help moving some boxes. He mumbled something about 'female musculature' and left. "I meant to ask," I stopped him, "do you know who's relieving me?"

"It was my understanding you are." That meant a double-shift. Nobody had said anything about that. "Is that a problem?"

"I guess I could use the money."

"As long as it suits your needs." After he left I turned to Terri. "I guess forensics attracts a few assholes, too."

Her face stiffened. She said, "He's my father."

My jaw must have dropped to the floor. Then she said, "Just kidding." We both laughed, a great feeling after all the stress and creepiness of the past week. I asked her where the boxes were she needed help with. "What boxes?" She smiled at me on her way out. For the first time, I was happy I'd come back to the island.

I grabbed a walkie from the office and did my rounds, a full perimeter around the island that took about an hour, give or take. Everything was fine, of course, and in the daylight it was almost an enjoyable time, like a normal, brisk walk on a rocky shore. At the high point of the island I even tried to look down below for the cave opening, but the tide was too high. I was starting to think Eric made that up anyway. Along the way I only saw one body, in a cage near the shore. Probably studying the effects of the ocean water or something like that. I stopped looking when I saw what was crawling out of its ear.

When I got back to the guard's office I stepped inside and looked around. Nothing out of place. Quiet. Just when I was about to sit down, I glanced into the break area. The cork board. The photo. Greg smiling awkwardly into the camera. Greg who might still be on this island, but not smiling. Not alive. I remembered why I was here, why I was really here, and this time it wasn't for the paycheck.

In case I don't come back, I wrote all this down to let you know that I'm going out right now and I'm going to get some answers. My first stop- that storage room.

4.

Things are much worse out here than I thought. I barricaded myself into the guard's office using the desk and the break room table. I'm covered in things I can't even think about and I don't know what to do. If I die out here it's my own damn fault. Damn it, why did I come back?

I have to stick to the story. People have to know what happened.

I went to the storage room like I said I would. It had all these boxes. I was really careful to be as quiet as possible, to make sure no one saw me go in, not into the research building and definitely not into that storage room, but someone must have seen me. That or a silent alarm. Maybe that's it. I started going through the boxes and at first it was what it was supposed to be, cleaned up skeletons separated and broken down to be shipped out, but I had to keep looking, didn't I?

In the back of the room I found a few boxes sealed up with orange tape and labeled to be put in the incinerator. I cut them all open and put the knife back in my pocket before I started looking inside them. The first one had random clothing inside. It took me a second, but I realized it was the clothing the bodies had shown up in. They stripped most of them before they laid them out. The box was a little creepy but nothing suspicious. Not until I opened the second box.

The first shirt I pulled out was a kind I knew too well. I knew it because I was wearing one just like it. It was a guard's uniform shirt, and it didn't stop at one. The whole box was filled with uniform shirts and pants. Black socks and shoes and belts, too. I counted four, five, six uniforms and as I pulled out each one my heart pounded louder. So loud I didn't hear someone enter the room behind me.

They must have snuck up on me and hit me over the head, because in an instant everything went black. I woke up with my back on cold rocks and the ocean screaming in my ears. The way my legs and arms felt I must have been injected with something, it was more druggy and numb than a concussion, and as my eyes tried to focus I started to make out the shapes of toothy rocks overhead. My wrists were tied behind me and I could barely feel them pinned under my back.

The ceiling was all rock and barely ten feet above. There was almost no light but the little bit of it seemed to come from the same direction as the sound of ocean waves. I turned my head and it felt like dragging a bag of rocks. I found myself looking into the terrified eyes of Eric. Eric, the guard who I was told called out sick, was lying next to me in the dark. His face was stained from crying and he was mumbling to himself but I couldn't make out what it was. It sounded like, "Thatookim. Thatookim." My head was swimming so badly, I tried to ask him what was happening but I could barely form the words. Finally I managed to get them out and he only repeated his mumbling louder and louder until he was screaming and crying the words at me: "They took them! They took them!"

I was still disoriented, and I didn't understand what he was talking about, but I did my best to keep my eyes in focus and look down, where he was looking now, still screaming, and that's when I saw what he was talking about.

His feet. His feet were gone, cut off cleanly above the ankle with the stubs wrapped in bandages. It wasn't messy at all but clean, professional, and even as I looked down at the horrors flopping at the ends of Eric's legs, I knew my suspicions were true. No regular man had done this, a doctor had, a surgeon, someone too familiar with how the human body was put together and more importantly how it was taken apart.

The shock of the sight cleared my head. I tried my best to calm Eric down using only my voice, since the rest of me was bound, but it wasn't easy. He seemed to be hurting pretty bad. Eventually I got him to stop yelling long enough to ask him who did this and why. He was in a daze, retreating inside his own mind or about to pass out from the pain, but finally he said something.

"Trying. Trying to bring him back."

"Who? Who is he trying to bring back," I asked, but he was completely catatonic. He wasn't going to be any more help, and I knew I had to focus on getting out of there or I would end up like him or worse. First I would save myself and then I'd come back for him. But then I heard a voice, a woman's voice, that made my heart jump in pure relief.

"Are you okay," Terri asked. She shone a flashlight on us and I could see by its light she was upset. I was so happy to see her I must have cursed ten different ways while laughing. I told her to untie me before that fucking psycho doctor came back to finish the job, but she went around to Eric first. She had a scalpel in her other hand, perfect for cutting rope, and I was glad to see she was prepared. I told her if she untied me first I could help her with Eric. But she looked up at me, and with this blank expression I can't explain, she just said, "I'm sorry."

Before I could make a sound she stuck the blade in Eric's throat. Blood bubbled up and Eric gurgled wide-eyed, while all I could do was watch him struggle. It was too much. I turned my head and waited for the awful sounds to stop, and by the time I looked back, Eric was gone. My stomach clenched as I realized the one person I thought I could trust had just murdered a man in front of me.

"Thank you," Terri said to Eric's corpse. Her voice sounded so genuine, like she was talking to a friend. I screamed at her and asked her what she was thanking him for. "For donating his body," she answered, as if it was obvious. "Without donors like Eric, William can't come back."

"Who the fuck is William?" But as I said it, I already knew the answer.

"I told you my brother went to a facility like this one, but that wasn't the whole truth. It wasn't just like this one- it was this one. William is here. He's here and he needs me." Even in the dim light I saw the look in her eyes, like every emotion was fighting inside of her. "I can hear him calling out for help. I don't want to do these things but he needs my help. Don't you see? Not just any parts will do. The doctor needs the bodies for his research, but they stopped funding him. Neither of us could let that happen. So I helped him. I put all those ads out. I called the agencies. I got him what we both needed."

Her eyes were full of tears. I couldn't believe how completely she'd fooled me into thinking she was a nice, sweet girl and now it was so obvious she had lost her mind. But believe it or not she was still my best chance at getting out alive. "The doctor doesn't care about you or your brother. He's using you," I said.

"You think I don't know that? He has his reasons and I have mine. We both make sacrifices to save lives."

"That's correct, dear," a man said behind her. Doctor Christianson stepped into the light wearing a rubber apron, like a butcher at a meat processing plant. "Sacrifices are always needed in the name of science." His mood was nonchalant, as if it was another day at the office. I told him he'd never get away with this, that someone would come looking into the disappearances, that they'd wonder what he was still doing out here after they cut his funding. "You're more right than you know. By next week this facility will sadly be shut down." He was saying it as much to Terri as he was to me.

Terri didn't take the news well at all. She got in his face, freaked out on him, shouted how William wouldn't be finished by next week, which honestly I didn't know what it meant and I didn't want to know, but he calmly told her the situation was unavoidable. He reminded her there was still time to finish what they'd started. When he said it, he looked over at me. Terri turned her attention back to me and she...I don't even want to say this, but she smiled at me. Smiled like she was still flirting with me. Meanwhile I was lying in Eric's spreading blood.

"You really do have kind eyes," she said, "just like William."

She came back and bent over me with the scalpel squeezed between her fingers. What she didn't know was I had a blade of my own, the knife which I'd managed to get out of my back pocket and was using to work on the rope around my wrists. I cut myself a few times with it, but nothing serious. I tried not to show it on my face as she came in closer. She smiled sadly as she brought the scalpel to my face. "He'll be happy to have his eyes back."

But suddenly the doctor was over her, and before either of us could react he stuck a hypodermic needle full of something pinkish into her neck and squeezed. She fell off me and immediately began to shake and spasm on the floor. The pained sounds that came out of her mouth were sickening. The doctor said, "Relax, dear. Thousands of people are embalmed every day."

I realized what he meant- the needle, it was filled with embalming fluid and God knows what else. I can't imagine what it must do to a living person, but based on Terri's reaction, the foam in her mouth, the sound of her swallowing her tongue, it didn't look good. The bastard was cleaning up his mess, and I refused to be a part of it. Refused to be another body for his farm. That's why as he was distracted watching Terri writhe on the floor, with his back to me, I finished cutting the rope around my wrist and did the same for the one around my ankles.

With everything in me I jumped on the unsuspecting prick and drove the small knife into his back. He cried out and collapsed under me and we both fell to the rocky floor. I pulled the knife out of him and prepared to stab him again, but a bright flash blinded me and a loud boom echoed so loudly in the thin space that I went deaf and felt my knees buckle and the knife fall out of my hand. It was a gunshot, a wild shot in the dark from a gun I hadn't seen in his hands. He had been about to finish off Terri when I jumped on him.

Completely disoriented, I stumbled away from the doctor and into the dark. Soon I was stepping into freezing cold water, ocean water, and I fell into it and pulled myself through the dark toward the faint moonlight and I didn't stop pulling until I emerged from the rocks and into the night.

How long had I been out? There was no time to think about it. I pulled myself up the rocky, wavy shore and up and onto the island where I found myself standing above the mouth of the cave. It seemed Eric hadn't been lying about it after all.

Eric. That poor bastard.

Not about to wait for the doctor to follow me out- and knowing that there was another way out of that cave, considering both Terri and the doctor's clothes had been dry- I did the smartest thing I've done all day: I ran. I wish I could say I jumped into the water and swam and swam until I reached the shore, but the ocean was too choppy and I've heard too many stories growing up around here of people drowning in the ocean at night. The undertows have claimed too many people for me to make a move like that.

I followed the shoreline at first, to make sure I didn't get lost in the trees, but soon I heard the doctor's voice calling out and his footsteps pounding the ground somewhere far behind me. Something bad was still in my blood, making my head groggy and my legs feel soft and distant, and where normally I could easily outrun him, I could hear him start to gain on me. With no choices left, I turned and ran into the woods.

My coordination was all wrong, and more than once I tripped on roots and slammed into trees, but I kept running. Even as his voice got closer and his footsteps louder I kept running. Soon my nose filled up with the dead smell and I came across a caged body between two trees. The man had been obese in life, and in death he was a crawling mound of putrid fat lying on its side. At that moment the doctor called out to me again, his voice so close now, and I knew he had that gun and those needles and who knows what else, and so I did the only thing I could think of, which was also the worst thing I could think of.

I lifted the cage and crawled in, and I was immediately hit with the powerful smell of the rotting man. There was no time to think. I let the cage back down and wedged myself in next to the cold corpse. I grabbed him by the arm and pulled him over me like an oozing blanket. As much as I could, I shut my nose and mouth tight, but there was only so much I could do. Its fluids leaked down onto me and maggots tumbled down into my hair, onto my clothes, down the collar of my shirt.

Footsteps. The doctor was walking past me. Past us. I held my breath for what felt like years as he continued on past and into the woods, even as something with a thousand tiny legs crawled over my neck and behind my ear. When I was sure the doctor was gone, I carefully, slowly pushed the huge corpse off me and got out of the cage. I shook the maggots off, took three steps and threw up until there was nothing left to throw up.

I ran in a different direction than I'd heard the doctor go, and by some miracle I found my way to the docks where I had prayed to find a boat of some kind, something either of them had used to get to the island, but my prayers weren't answered. There was no time to cry about it, though, because I had one goal and one goal only: to get to that radio and call for help. Call for police. Call the army. Call anyone to come out here and get me. I wasn't screwing around anymore.

I barricaded myself into the office by locking the door, then flipping over the desk and shoving it against the door. Then I took the table from the break area, flipped it long side up and pushed it against the window. When I went into the room where the radio was kept, something like hope died in me.

The radio was destroyed.

I came back out, went to the computer and started writing this because I don't know how else to tell people what happened out here. When the doctor gets here I'll give him hell, and I intend to beat the med school brains out of him, but in case he gets the better of me I need the world to know what went down on this island, and I just...

My god, the most terrifying thing. I just looked up to see the doctor staring at me through the door's window. I ran into the other room to find something to hit him with in case he gets in, but then there was this horrible sound, I can't even describe it, wet shrieking, and then these red lights started coming through the windows and the doctor started screaming, brutal, terrified screams, like something was attacking him, and he fired his gun two, three times, and then it sounded like whatever it was got to him because he screamed and then his voice cut out. It's...

It's beating on the door now. The red light, it won't stop. What is it? What is it?

Listen, I'm writing this because I have no phone and no one to email. My father is dead and my mother might as well be. I have no friends and no one to help me. Don't come out here, I'll update tomorrow. I'll be okay. I'll think of something. God, just don't come out here. Before I sign off, I have something to confess. I was

5.

I don't know how to start this except to say I'm sorry. I'm sorry because I have almost no memory of the things I wrote, or even of writing them at all.

Three days ago I woke up in the hospital looking like I'd taken a brisk jog through one of the circles of Hell. I had no idea how I'd gotten here or what happened to me, but from the looks of it, it seemed like I'd been attacked by an animal of some kind. There were cuts and bruises all over my body and a pretty bad hematoma had colored my right eye red. I knew who I was and all that, but my last solid memory was of job searching after leaving my old job. After that it gets blurry. It's a bit like trying to remember what your third grade teacher looked like.

The nurses have been nice to me, and extremely patient with what I can only describe as my overall confusion with life, but whenever I ask them what happened they have no real answers. The only information I got out of them was that I'd been found wandering around near the shore, bloody and disoriented, and when someone tried to approach me to ask if I needed help, I nearly clawed the poor guy's eyes out. From there your guess is as good as mine, but I'm pretty sure it involved some cops and a handcuffed ambulance ride. Apparently they tested me for drugs and found a bouquet of narcotics in my system. A bouquet. Their words, not mine.

Two days ago one of my neighbors was nice enough to pick up a few things from my apartment, one of which was my laptop. As far as my phone goes, who knows what happened to that thing, it's at the bottom of the ocean as far as I know. Having my laptop is nice, though. I use it to kill time while I wait to get out of the hospital, and also to send my mother an email telling her I was okay. She didn't respond, of course, but at least I did my part. My conscience is clean.

You can imagine my surprise when I opened the page titled "The Body Farm" and found all these things I'd written just days ago about an island full of corpses. I've never experienced anything like this, but my head was flooded with pictures- small moments, bits of faces, both alive and dead, snippets of conversations like sound bites on the news. Each piece was cut too short to make any sense. It felt, honestly, like a dream, something I'd made up to entertain myself, except that some of the pictures felt too real, too grounded to be a dream. I read every word of it. If I blinked more than twice in that time, I'd be impressed.

It's a strange feeling having that kind of distance from something that happened to you. I felt like one of those people who yells at horror movies, except the actor on the screen looked exactly like me. I wondered why on Earth I would go back to that island, not just once but twice, and how I could be so naive about the doctor. I formed opinions and took guesses as to what the truth was- I'm pretty sure all that missing body and handprint stuff was Terri running around the island being generally insane-

and became frustrated with how it ended. That confession bit? I really wish I knew what I was about to say there. Just ten seconds more and the truth would have come out. Maybe it's better that I don't know, now that I survived and all, but as they say- the truth always comes out in the end.

Yesterday was a bad day. The pain was stronger than normal, so the morning nurse gave me an extra dose of morphine along with all the other antibiotics and various meds they have me on. It helped to dull the pain, but with it the rest of me was dulled, too. The whole day I felt like I was being held under warm water, watching the bodies float past, never quite close enough to touch them. It took me a minute to understand what the nurse was saying when she said someone was there to see me, if it was okay with me. All I could say was, "Can't everyone see me?" I mean, had I died and become a ghost? Did they need to ask my permission for me to appear? I said yes, of course, they could see me, and a minute later I was looking at a hand holding a badge, and someone was telling me his name was Detective Andrews and he wanted to ask some questions.

I took a minute to sit up, drink some water and shake off the fog. I apologized to the young detective and told him he looked familiar. He was surprised and said he'd actually tried to speak to me a few days earlier but I'd been too out of it to hold a conversation. "You were beat up pretty badly," he said, "can you remember anything from the attack?"

So it's true I was attacked.

"That's what it appears. That's why I'm here. Do you have any reason to think otherwise?" I told him I was pretty sure I was attacked, but I was having a hard time sorting out exactly what it was that had attacked me. He could tell I was holding out on him.

"I don't want to force you to relive a traumatic event," he said, "but if you know something you're not telling me, I have to insist for the sake of the investigation." After a few moments I got my laptop from the side table, opened the bookmark and spun it to face him.

"You have to read the whole thing," I told him. He looked confused, but he agreed. A little while later he closed the laptop and handed it back to me.

"You can't actually believe this."

I'm not sure what I believed, I told him, but a few facts remained: one, I had been attacked by someone or something incredibly violent, and two, some of my memories coincided with the events in the story. He was skeptical, but he said he would look into it on the off chance that parts of the story were based on real events I had distorted. "The brain has a funny way of taking creative licenses," he said.

Before he left I gave him all the details I could drum up and told him his best bet was tracking down some of those interns who had worked on the island. He told me I was better off not sharing the story with anyone else, including strangers on the internet, for the sake of the investigation. I assured him I had no interest in having people look at me like I was sick in the head, especially when I told them a murderous doctor and a girl with a ghost brother were trying to kill me.

This morning the phone by the side of my bed rang. It was Detective Andrews saying he'd found Doctor Christianson's name attached to the island, but that the university had cut ties with the doctor a number of months ago. He went on to say that records of the interns who had worked on the body farm were sloppy at best. As of yet he'd had no luck tracking any of them down.

But it got better. He also informed me that the police had found no evidence of foul play on the island other than signs it had served as a body farm very recently, a fact on common record, and that any clue to the doctor's whereabouts led invariably to a dead end.

A dead end. His words.

Here's the final kicker: he asked me if I would go with him to the island. He wants me to show him around the place, take him through the story and maybe even point out where they should be digging for clues. After saying no about nine or ten different ways, and him saying it was the best chance at finding who had hurt me, I agreed on two conditions. One, we would arrive on the island during the day and leave before it got dark. And two, we would have a full police escort the entire time we were there. The actual words I used were "a butt-load of cops," but the meaning was all the same.

He accepted my conditions. We go in three days, the day I get out of this hospital.

6.

I don't know who I can believe anymore, if anyone at all. My days have become a surreal series of events, and I find myself questioning everything that happens within them. Even my own thoughts.

After I checked myself out of the hospital I caught a cab to my place, good old apartment 403, and proceeded to take the longest shower of my life. It was probably the greatest feeling I've ever known, with a close second going to the nap I took directly after. I passed out for a long time, the kind of deep, heavy sleep that feels like it will last the rest of your life. The only reason I woke up was because someone rang my doorbell. It turned out to be Detective Andrews. He saw by my face that I'd been sleeping and apologized for not being able to call before he came over.

I still have to remember to buy a new phone when I get a chance.

We took the short drive to the shore in the detective's car without saying much. I double-checked that we wouldn't be going to the island alone, and he assured me several other detectives would be meeting us on the pier. First he said he wanted to bring me to the boat launch, in case it jogged my memory. I also suspected it was to see how the boat owner reacted to my presence, but we were both in for a surprise when we stepped inside the small launch office.

The guy behind the counter was young, not what I'd described in my writings at all. He turned out to be the launch's new owner.

He explained to us that the old owner, Willis, had sold it to him for dirt cheap, which is how it changed hands so quickly. He had no information about Willis' whereabouts but he did know that the old man had sold the business after the boat captain, who was apparently his brother, had urged him to. He said they'd seemed pretty nervous about something. "Maybe it was something they saw," I told Andrews. He nodded but didn't say anything. Before we left I asked if Willis had left anything behind, a cell phone maybe, but the young guy said he hadn't found anything.

We got back in the detective's car and drove a few minutes to a different pier, where two more detectives met us by a boat on one of the docks. One was blonde and named Detective Cooper. The other had red hair and a mustache and was called Detective Bennett. They didn't seem familiar to me at all, which offered me a weird kind of relief. I asked to see their badges, which they showed me, and they seemed amused when I studied them closely. "My new year's resolution is to be less trusting," I offered. They didn't laugh. When I asked where the rest of the cops were they explained that they were already out on the island. We all got in the boat and headed over. Cooper was at the wheel.

The weather was nice, one of those first days of Spring that make the Winter feel like a bad dream, but at the back of my mind, nagging me, was a voice of dread. It couldn't believe I was going back to that damn island. As much as I bitch and complain about it, whenever I'm given the chance to return to Twain

Island I always take it. Maybe something about it calls to me. I don't know. Meanwhile the detectives were having quiet conversations without me, just under the sound of the motor and the slapping of the boat against the ocean, and when I leaned in closer they stopped talking.

As we came close to the island I felt a ball form in my stomach and a sharp pain in my temples. I noticed there weren't any boats tied to the dock. "Calm down," Andrews told me. "They'll be here."

"You promised me a butt-load of cops," I said.

"The police have cases other than yours. Now relax. The three of us are more than capable of keeping you safe."

I argued with him a bit more, but in the end there was nothing to talk about. We were already at the island and it was too late to turn around. I told them I'd decided to stay on the boat until they got back. Detective Cooper took the keys with him as he got out of the boat. Bennett pointed out that I'd be alone if I stayed behind. I didn't like his tone, like an adult threatening a kid with the boogie man. Andrews was the most understanding. He said he understood my hesitation, and normally they wouldn't expect a victim to return to the scene of an incident, but as it stood I was both the only witness and the only evidence they had. Without my help, whatever had happened on that island would stay a mystery for good. And that meant whoever had attacked me would go free while I lived in fear.

He had a good point.

The first stop we made was to the guard's office. As we came up the small hill, and I saw the state of the building, I felt immediate validation. The door had clearly been smashed in, half of it dangling on its frame and the other half spread in shards across the floor. The detectives stepped inside first. After a second of hesitation, I followed.

There was a strong smell in the air I couldn't place. The scene was exactly how I'd described it, the desk and table on their sides where they'd been used to barricade the door, but the computer I'd used to type all those entries was missing, along with the broken two-way radio in the other room. When I asked the detectives if they'd been removed as evidence, they said neither of those items had been found. "Then I guess someone did a bit of clean-up before the cops arrived," I said.

That was when I realized what the smell was- bleach.

"Someone did a thorough job of scrubbing the island," Detective Bennett said. He said whoever it was had missed a few drops of blood, and he pointed to the spot where they'd been found, high up on the far wall. It had to have been a brutal attack for any amount of blood to make it that far. I asked if the blood had been tested, to see who it belonged to, and he said they were still waiting for lab results.

"I have a feeling it's mine," I said.

"At least some of it," he replied. I noticed him exchange an uncomfortable glance with the other men, like he'd said too much, and suddenly it hit me: was I a suspect? From their perspective I was the guy who'd been found bloody and high, with stories of strange lights and disappearing corpses. A single, white male who was recently unemployed. My god, I fit the bill. But did they really think I'd go back there if I was responsible for what happened? Then again, the criminal supposedly always returns to the scene of the crime.

If the guard's office was cleaned out, the main research facility made it look like Exhibit A in comparison. Every box, every machine, every instrument had disappeared from the building, neatly packed up and taken away in the time since I'd been there. My memories from the island were still spotty at best, but I had distinct images in my mind of what those places had looked and felt like, and what I was seeing didn't match up. Where before it had been an active place of research, what we stood in now was a shell, a hollow building on a silent island. Somehow it had become even eerier without the boxes full of dead bones and skulls. Lonelier, maybe.

From there we began a walk around the island. The detectives let me take the lead- not walking in front, mind you, just pointing the direction we should go- and I did my best to guess and feel my way from body site to body site. At each one we found only the telltale patches of flattened, dead grass which marked where a body had been laid out. A few of them reminded me of snow angels. Not even the wire cages which had held most of the bodies were left behind, and I was more and more amazed by the thoroughness of the clean-up job.

Eventually I led the detectives to where the entrance of the cave should have been, but not being low tide it wasn't visible down below. With their help I scoured the nearby area for any signs of a second entrance, which I was still sure had to be there, but after close to an hour we'd turned up nothing to speak of but a few, rusted batteries and an empty bottle of booze.

"There's nothing here," Detective Bennett said, sounding annoyed. Cooper and Andrews looked at me, waiting for me to say something. I shrugged and told them to come back during low tide. Without another word they turned and started heading back toward the boat.

As I trailed the men back through the forest, the headache which had settled into my temples as we approached the island, and had been there in the background since, expanded through the back of my skull until it became a full-on migraine. As someone not prone to migraines it was an intense feeling- the sunlight and the sound of the ocean became unbearable. Even smells seemed to grow stronger, which on that island was not a good thing. My eyes watered and felt like they wanted to burst out of their sockets. I stopped walking, trying to push the pain back, but the detectives ahead were totally oblivious.

As I stood there holding my nauseous stomach, I saw someone move between the trees. Plain as day, it was a human figure. In the forest. In the distance.

I shouted out to the detectives but from their angle they couldn't see him. I was fed up with the whole situation. I don't care how crazy it sounds but I ran full-speed into the forest, chasing the man I'd seen in the distance. The detectives followed after me as I weaved between the trees, yelling for the stranger to stop. Only once I caught another glimpse of him but then he was gone, disappeared just past a grouping of trees.

No matter how fast I ran I couldn't catch him again, and eventually the detectives shouted for me to stop. They looked for footprints in the dirt but found only mine. Not one of them had seen him, and I couldn't tell if they believed me or were just humoring me. The description I gave them of the man was vague, and I decided to keep it that way.

In the boat again, heading back to shore, I caught a glimpse of a birthmark on Detective Andrews' neck, just behind his ear. It sounds strange, but the sight of it sent the biggest sense of deja vu up my spine, and I knew in that moment that I hadn't recognized him from the hospital, that I had to have met him sometime before that.

"So what happened to the other officers," I asked. "The ones who were supposed to meet us out here."

Cooper shouted over the noise of the motor. "We had to get you out to the island somehow."

After we got to shore, Cooper and Bennett went their own way and Andrews dropped me off back at my apartment. Before he could pull away, I leaned back in and asked which precinct he and the other detectives worked for. "Thirty-first," he said.

I was quiet a second. "You're full of shit, aren't you?"

Without responding he put the car into drive and pulled away. I should have written down his plate number, but I didn't think of it until it was too late. When I got inside I looked up the thirty-first precinct and called them up using my neighbor's phone. Not surprisingly, no one by those names works for the police.

The more I think about it, the more I recognized the stranger I saw out on the island. I'd gotten a better look at him that I let on, but I wasn't about to tell the "detectives" that unless I wanted to spend some time in a mental ward.

The man in the forest- it was me.

7.

I don't know why I bothered getting a new phone. I've been finding it so hard to concentrate lately, I can barely hold down a conversation. My thoughts often start in one place and end up somewhere completely different, to the point where I can't remember what I'd been thinking of in the first place. The other day I managed to land a phone interview for a pretty decent job, but halfway through the call I lost track of my words so badly, I actually forgot what the question was. I tried my best to recover but it was too late. The woman thanked me for my time and got off the phone as quickly as she could. Not surprisingly, she didn't call back. I hate these phone interviews, anyway. People half my intelligence, judging me from a thousand miles away. They're lucky we're not in the same room so I can't slap the clipboard out of their hands.

What was I saying?

The phone. I got a new phone with my first unemployment check. I told the kid at the store they should replace it for free, but he said I hadn't gone for the extra insurance so I had to pay for a new one. This kid couldn't have been a day over twenty and he gets to bully me into spending a chunk of my unemployment on something I already bought. He wanted me to upgrade my contract, too, until I got loud with him. He dropped the sales pitch pretty quickly after that.

I'm doing it again. The point is, someone keeps calling me and hanging up. At first I thought it was a problem with the new phone, but then I called the number back and heard breathing on the other end. It wasn't lewd or anything, more, I don't know, panicked. After listening to it a few seconds I got pissed off and said, "Hello? Who is this?" There was a loud sound like whoever it was slammed their phone down and then the line cut out. They haven't called back since, but I'm still waiting.

It's not just the phone calls. Last night I was woken up by a knock on the door in the middle of the night. When I answered it, no one was there. No one at my door, no one in the hallway. I got to the door pretty quick, too, quicker than it takes for the elevator to come up from the lobby. There's a stairwell they could have taken down, but the door squeaks so loudly, I definitely would have heard someone open it.

So either one of my neighbors knocked on my door at two in the morning, or the invisible man.

I've called the police, more than once, but they're no help. They came out to my apartment and took my statement about Andrews and the other fake detectives, but they didn't seem too convinced by my story. Whenever I ask about the attack that put me in the hospital they say the case is "pending further evidence," which is a nice way of saying it's closed. I won't give up, though. I called and I called until finally one officer said, "Look, my guess is you got loaded on tranquilizers and hurt yourself." These are the people who are supposed to be protecting me. He said I'm lucky no one pressed charges for assault or property damage. I'm lucky. His words.

My neighbor Pete, the guy who visited me in the hospital, said a detective came around asking about me. I tried to explain that the person he talked to probably wasn't a real detective, but now the guy wants nothing to do with me. I even caught the woman across the hall staring, so I can only assume either word got around or the "detective" paid more than one visit in the building. As far as lawyers go, you can forget it. The only guys interested in my case are the kind of bottom-scrapers and ambulance chasers I would never hire in the first place.

I couldn't sleep last night, so I got dressed and left the building to go for a walk. My thoughts were racing so badly, like two people arguing over each other, but the wind felt good on my skin, and before I knew it I was taking a booth at the Lighthouse Diner a couple of miles from my apartment. They know me enough there to get a few head nods from the employees, but not so much that they know my name or what I do. Sometimes that's best- they don't know my business, and I don't know theirs.

The waitress came over to take my order. "No friends tonight," she asked.

"Just me." I ordered a coffee and an omelette. I don't like eggs much, but I've been craving them lately. I've been craving a lot of weird things. The waitress put my order in and dropped off the coffee, leaving me to prepare it alone in the empty diner. As I poured the sugar in, I casually glanced over at my reflection in the mirrored wall across the aisle.

I wasn't alone in the booth.

The man seated across from me was immediately recognizable as Andrews, or whatever his actual name is, dressed in clothes that weren't trying to make him look like a detective. I understood right away that I wasn't seeing a ghost or anything like that. It was a memory, a slice of something forgotten coming through. The cuts and bruises on my face were gone, or rather not there yet. Even my clothes weren't the same, and I was struck with the fear that if I moved my head, even slightly, the spell would be broken and the memory would be lost forever. I could see from my peripherals that no one was actually seated at the booth with me. The effect it had on my vision was completely disorienting.

By the movement of his lips, the memory of Andrews was talking to the memory of me, though I couldn't hear a word of it. The birthmark on his neck could be seen from my angle, as well as a yellow folder on the table between us. For a moment, the sound of the memory fluttered through my ears. Just five words of Andrews' voice:

"You have to go back."

Overcome with curiosity, and worried the memory would fade before I got any answers, I slowly, slowly turned my head to look down at the table, hoping the folder would still be there. But there was only my coffee. A second later my food arrived, further breaking the spell. I ate my eggs in silence and when I was done I asked for the bill. Before she left the table, I reached out and stopped the waitress. "Quick question," I said. "What did you mean when you said 'no friends tonight'?"

"Aw, hey, I wasn't trying to be mean," she pouted in a friendly way.

"It's fine- did you say that because the last time I came here I was with someone?"

"The last few times, I think."

"Did you happen to catch his name, or see it on his credit card, anything like that?"

She shook her head. "He paid cash if I remember. Why, did something happen?"

I waved the question off. "Nothing you would believe." She nodded, looking a bit weirded out. I paid the bill and headed home. This time I really felt the distance. The night reminded me of the island, the way the wind whistled in the treetops, making me feel hollow. By the time I got home I was cold and drowsy and tired of walking, but even still, when I laid down in bed to give sleep another shot, I could feel it wasn't going to happen anytime soon.

After the first hour of lying awake in bed, I began to hear sounds. Whispers in the dark, but wet, like they were shaped from the sounds of maggots shifting. I jumped up, turned on the lights and checked every corner of the apartment. Nothing was there.

When I finally did fall asleep, I dreamt of being a kid again. I was back home with a living father and a mother who spoke to me, and they were good dreams, of holidays and playing and dinner time, but whenever I would turn my head, the house, the sky, everything, was lit in a deep, red light.

8.

This can't be real. I know this can't be real.

Two days ago I decided to leave town, for good. Too many people who couldn't be trusted knew where I lived. The way I figured it, you only get one life, so you'd better make it last as long as possible. If I had to wander the country, be homeless or join the circus, at least I'd be alive. There was nothing left for me back in that town, anyway- no friends, no family, no job. I might as well start over somewhere new, somewhere nobody knows me, and pray my problems don't follow me there.

I drove for as long as I could. There was no destination in mind, just west, like the old pioneers, except instead of fighting dysentery I only had to stop every few hundred miles for gas. I drove until I could barely keep my eyes open, and the first time I nodded off I picked out the cheapest motel I could find and checked in. A sickly girl with small teeth gave me a key and told me where to find ice, though she didn't sound too convinced of it herself. My head barely touched the pillow before I was asleep. Except here's the thing: I fell asleep in a motel bed, that much I know.

But I woke up on the island.

Sunlight danced on the leaves. It was a bright day, too bright for my eyes, as if they were adjusting to the light after walking out of a darkened theater, but it wouldn't go away no matter how long I waited. The sun was angry on my skin, and I felt about the light a way I never had before. It bothered me. Hurt me. Right away I suspected I was dreaming, but it all felt too real- the feel of the grass underfoot, the salty air that stung at my nostrils. Over to my left was the dock, with no boat as usual, and behind me the main research building and the guard's office. As I studied them, dumbfounded, I noticed they were in perfect condition. The guard's office especially was intact, no busted down door or damage of any kind.

And there were voices coming from inside.

Slowly I walked between the buildings to the side of the guard's office, giving distance to the windows, careful not to be seen, and pressed my ear to the wall. The voices were muted but familiar-sounding, and I struggled to make out the words.

A laugh, one I would know anywhere. It was Eric, the day guard. Eric, laughing. Eric, alive. Hearing him like that set something off inside me, and I took my ear from the wall and headed toward the door. I'd like to say it was relief at hearing him alive, or some heroic need to warn him about his coming death, but to be honest, more than anything, I felt angry. A rage boiled up in my center as I took step after step through the grass. But before I could reach the door it opened, and someone stepped out into the daylight, closing the door behind them.

Terri.

I'd gone over this scenario in my head a thousand times, what I would do if I could get my hands on her, this psycho, this black widow, how I would enjoy making her pay for what she'd done to me and so many other unsuspecting men. I never thought I'd actually get that chance, considering she'd died back in that cave, but these days, all things considered, that doesn't seem to change anything.

As I bore down on her I said her name. Terri, alive, Terri, smiling, she looked up at me, and I saw her eyes wash over with emotion- fear and pain and something else, something wrong- and she glanced back at the office to check that the door was closed before she spoke.

"What are you doing here?"

"Looking for you," I replied, my throat hoarse. She looked again at the door. As I advanced on her she didn't back down, didn't try to fight, she only stepped forward and said something I couldn't hear. In my mind all I wanted to do was grab her, to hit her, choke her, shake the life from her. But the moment I reached out, hands going for her, my eyes went dark.

Night. I stood on the dock listening to the ocean. It was an eternal sound that pulled at my gut, urging me to step off the wood and into the water. The coastline with its lights and sounds seemed the most foreign, most unnatural thing to me at that moment.

There were closer lights, too. The guard's office was lit up like a torch in the night for the moths to bump and spiral against, not just the outer, security lights but the ones inside the windows as well. But there was something more important I had noticed, not a light but a sound, out in the trees past the buildings: the sound of a man walking through the woods.

Quietly, trying not to give myself away, I left the dock behind and walked up the hill past the office, past the bright window where inside the computer clicked and hummed. I tracked the sound in the trees through the first clearing- my God, the rotting bodies were back, even the disappearing and reappearing woman- and halfway across the island, always keeping my distance in case my footsteps were too heavy. I felt clumsy in the dark, uncoordinated, and I didn't want to be heard by whoever it was I was trailing.

Based on the direction they were going, I had a pretty good idea who it was.

A few hundred yards from where the pretend detectives and I had searched for the elusive second cave entrance, I doubled my pace without care for the noise. I'd be damned if I lost the bastard now. Yet damned I apparently was, because as I came to where the entrance should have been, I found myself very much alone in the clearing, staring out at ivy and leaves soaked in dew. I didn't see much choice except to wait, so I dug myself in behind an elm and watched carefully for anything unusual, any sight or sound to go on.

It took less than five minutes. With no warning a patch of thick, thick ivy swung up from the ground less than twenty feet from where I crouched. The ivy was mounted to a buried door, the wood made up to look like dirt, the whole thing so dirty and ivy-tangled we'd missed it on every pass. Doctor Christianson rose up from the ground. He calmly climbed an unseen ladder then stepped up from the depths and onto the ground. He shut the door behind him and tossed something into the tall grass, stomping back into the woods. I waited until he was gone, then scrambled forward and checked what he'd thrown.

A mostly empty bottle of whiskey, the remains dribbling into the dirt. I left it and pushed my hands into the wet ivy, searched around until my fingers found a handle. The hidden door lifted so easily, and once it was propped open on its rusted hinge I clambered down the hole beneath, feet slipping on the cold metal rungs of the ladder that led down into the ground.

The sea echoed against rock, and there was just enough light for me to stumble my way through the cave. It wasn't the moon, or a candle or a flashlight that guided me, but the blinking, cycling lights of machines working in the dark that drew me in. One or two had small monitors, but most of them were of an older style, with dials and diodes and paper-fed read-outs and a crowd of other things I've never seen outside of a black-and-white movie, and one of the screens showed a topographic line-map of land which could only be Twain Island, with small bulbs inserted in key points. One of them was lit up and buzzing, and if I had to guess I would put its location somewhere close to where Greg's body was. Greg, the guy with the arms.

As I got closer to the busy machines, one of them, the largest, clicked on as if responding to company, and a large, thick-glassed bulb at its top, one that reminded me of the lamp and lens at the top of a lighthouse, hummed to life. The filament inside glowed hot and then hotter and somewhere a paper feed began spitting out lengths. The glass was red and so was the light. The sight of it sucked me in even stronger than the ocean had not long before.

I reached out for it, reached for the expanding glow, walked toward the welcoming, luminescent red, and in the throbbing crimson light I could see there was something wrong with my hand near the thumb, something that didn't belong there, and as all became the dark warmth of red sun, I made out the faint patterns of black thread stitched into my skin.

I woke up in the morning, in my car, pulled over at a harsh angle on the side of road. Whether I'd stayed in a motel or not I couldn't say, but enough cash was missing from my wallet that I think I did.

These days it's so hard to keep track of every, little thing. It's bad enough keeping track of where I am, let alone where I've been.

Back on the island, when I reached for Terri, she'd said something I couldn't hear. I've spent a lot of time since thinking about her lips, the way they moved, the words they formed. The three words she'd said. I think I know what they were now.

"You're not finished."

The last few days before I left town, I'd started having blackouts, long periods of time I lost track of. My car wouldn't be where I'd parked it. Food would be gone from my refrigerator. Before I left, I made one, last stop. I drove to the employment agency who put me on that damn island in the first place. I wanted to question the prick who ran it. I needed to know if he was in on it, if he'd knowingly sent me and God knows how many others into the snake pit, or if he'd been as naive as I was. But when I got there all I found was the charred remains of a building. What was left of it was marked off with police tape.

Someone had burned it to the ground.

9.

Quiet days at the bank are nice sometimes, but they do have a tendency to drag unless I keep busy. That's really why I started writing stories in the first place. They're my little distractions from the silence and the other things I'd rather not think about. So I was at my desk, taking advantage of the quiet by catching up on some paperwork, when suddenly I had this powerful feeling, this realization that what was happening, all of this, was wrong.

It began to sink in that I shouldn't be there, that I hadn't worked there in weeks and more disturbingly couldn't remember how I'd gotten there. Was it all a dream? And if so, had I woken up?

"Hey." I tried to flag down a passing customer, but she didn't answer. She kept walking as if she hadn't heard me, and in fact no one was paying attention to me or doing anything but staring ahead or down at their work.

I wanted to get a look at the date, to get some kind of explanation for all this, but I couldn't get my computer monitor to turn on. I banged on the keyboard and clicked the mouse but nothing happened. Unresponsive. I gave the tower under my desk a hard kick and then the screen clicked on and began to buzz to life. Instead of the desktop, though, the screen was pure white. Then it changed, becoming pink at first and then darkening to a deep red. It was bright, almost blinding, and I tried to click the mouse again only to find there was no mouse and no keyboard under my hands. There wasn't even a tower, the one I just kicked.

I wheeled back from my desk with my hands in front of my eyes to shield them from the sting of the red light. It became so strong that it filled the entire bank, ceiling, walls and floor, from the desk cubicles to the teller window to the lobby at the far end, yet no one reacted in the slightest. They continued their work and went about their day, bathed in the light, oblivious to the blood color wrapping their eyes.

Up out of my chair I went to Carol, one of my co-workers, and called her name. She didn't look up. I did the same to Vince, and when he didn't respond to the name I repeated it louder. It was like talking into the wind- the sound of his name was sucked up into the vacuum. I went from desk to desk, banged on the security glass of the teller window and shouted as loud as I could from the center of the bank. Nothing was heard. Nothing was seen. Time had drained from the room, and I knew then I needed to escape before I drained down with it.

The door.

I ran through the lobby and out the door, needing to be free of that place. When I burst out of the building I expected to find the same gray parking lot I'd come out to hundred of times before, the flat stretch of cracked concrete broken by tall lights every twenty spaces, but instead I came out to a blur of brown and green and blue. When I stopped myself there was the sound of seagulls and crashing waves.

I was on the island again.

I turned around to look back at the bank but it was already gone, the entire six-story building vanished like it was never there. My chest seized up with a choking helplessness as I realized there was no way off this island, that no matter how fast I ran or how far I drove, the moment I turned my head it could all come crashing back. A chunk of rock surrounded by sea was always there, ready to squeeze me between cold fingers.

It was time to focus. Time to go home. Where was I on the island? Somewhere near the cave, as far as I could tell, but it was hard to be sure without landmarks. It was daytime but the woods all looked the same. I took my best guess at the direction of the dock and started off, amazed at how many times now I had taken this walk I'd sworn to never take. Not two minutes later, I heard a shout from far behind me.

It was a man's voice telling me to stop. Without a second thought or even a first, I ran. I ran like hell and didn't stop running no matter how much the unseen man ordered me to, until I spotted a thick grouping of trees up ahead and made a line for it, aiming for the small space between two large elms. I ran so fast I didn't feel my feet touch the dirt. The trees came up quickly and I ran between the two elms, hoping to lose what now sounded like three or four men chasing me through the woods.

I came out the other side in a long hallway that echoed with high-pitched sound. Going from outdoors to indoors with no transition at all was jarring, though I knew right away where I was. It was the main research building, the laboratories on the left and on the right were the cleaning and packing rooms I knew too well. There was no need to turn around. I knew the woods would be gone.

My ears adjusted to the echoes. The high-pitched sound was a woman crying.

It was coming from the packing room at the end of the hall, and as much as I didn't want to go any closer I was compelled to seek it out, maybe because the voice was familiar. It wasn't Terri's. It was someone older, and they sounded like they were in pain, and so I went forward, went toward the familiar and the painful.

When I turned the corner I'd expected to find the woman but all I found was the packing room, empty except for the boxes, stacks of bones and skulls. Yet the crying continued. The woman in pain, her voice, it formed wordless cries for help, painful and destroyed and reaching out for compassion. As I walked into the room it grew louder, closer, and it became obvious that the cries were coming from one of the boxes sitting on the work desk. It was sealed with tape. I could swear I could see it shaking.

I knew whose voice it was. The woman. I backed away and left her there, shutting the door behind me to muffle the cries.

On my way back up the hallway and toward the exit, I peeked into the laboratory on my right and caught sight of a familiar scene, familiar yet different. Three men in lab coats unwrapped a new corpse laid out on the metal slab, pulling a man's head free and peeling black plastic away from crusted skin. I stopped heading for the exit and approached the door, placed my palms on its window and watched the men work. It was like seeing some moment from a future time, echoing a moment from the past. I could only see the back of the laboratory men, but one of them had a birthmark on his neck just behind his ear.

When I looked again at the corpse they were unwrapping, I found its eyes were open and staring at me. It was Bernard. He was dead, drained of blood, yet I could still feel his hatred for me. His accusing eyes stayed unblinking on me as I turned away and left.

Standing in the guard's office, all of it pristine and unbroken except for the two-way radio, which wouldn't pick up a signal, I found I didn't know where to go anymore, where to run. I was at a crossroads.

Then I remembered: my phone was in my pocket. There'd been no boat launch to turn it in, I'd come straight from the bank where my phone was always on me. I fumbled it out of my pocket and tried calling the cops first. It rang and rang without answer. I hung up and tried calling the first number in my contacts. No answer. I dialed seven, random numbers and waited ten rings before giving up.

Just as I was about to put my phone away, it rang in my hand.

I answered it and brought it to my ear. My breathing was heavy, panicked, and as much as I tried to speak my throat was too tight to let the words out. After a few seconds, an annoyed voice on the other side said, "Hello? Who is this?"

Cold fear spread through me. The phone fell from my stiff hand and hit the floor, breaking into a million shards of glass and plastic that danced across the floor. The connection was lost.

Acid burned in my throat and my stomach felt ready to spill. I looked toward the bathroom but had to look again when I saw the door had changed. The location was the same but the type was entirely different, no longer a bathroom door but the door to an apartment. It even had a number plate screwed to it at eye level.

Apartment 403.

My apartment.

With my hand shaking I tried the handle but found it was locked. I checked my pockets for keys and came up empty. So I knocked. I knocked on my own door not knowing what to expect, if it would swing open and I would find myself face-to-face with myself or maybe someone else completely, living in my apartment, taking over my things. At this point nothing would surprise me. I waited a second. My hand hovered as I considering knocking again. I decided not to.

As I looked around at the office, trying to figure out where to go from there, if I should risk jumping in the rough ocean and making a swim for shore, I heard the unmistakable sound of the door shutting behind me. I swung around to see what had opened it, but there was only a closed door. Not my door, not apartment 403, it was only a bathroom door. I opened it, unlocked now, and looked inside to find the bathroom and nothing more.

I don't know where I am anymore. I'm not even sure I'm really writing this. I feel lost, exposed, like a hermit crab pulled from its shell. Some part of me is fading fast, and I'm afraid the next time I close my eyes, the next time I blink, it'll be for good.

I'm sorry, mom. I'm sorry about dad. You told me I would answer for my sins and you were right.

10.

"They didn't bury their treasure here- they buried their dead."

I was woken by a gunshot. The rough sounds of scuffles in the dark reverberated in my skull. It took a long time, too long, to draw enough energy to open my eyes, and twice as long to sit up, but finally my feet dangled from the slab. The contraption around my chest glowed faint red at its center, and grew brighter each time I moved.

My body was difficult to control. The skin felt twisted over bones, like I'd slept in a suit one size too small. The first time I stood up I fell down, hit the stone floor hard, but I stood up, steadied myself on an instrument table and eventually took my first step, followed by another, and then another. The stone was cold and damp under naked feet.

The cave was lit up by lanterns and the excited readouts of machines, all those computers cooling down from their purposes. However long I thought it had taken to open my eyes, my perception of time had been wrong. It seemed I was alone inside the cave; the fight had moved elsewhere.

Halfway across the cave, I found my sister. She lay in a ditch of wet rock like a lost doll. I fell on her and wiped the foam from her mouth to check her breathing. It was faint, the same for the pulse in her neck. There was a needle mark where a droplet of blood had beaded up. Before I could try to resuscitate her, her eyes fluttered open and she smiled up at me.

"Who did this to you?" My voice. It felt so strange coming out of my throat.

"Your eyes." She was raspy, strained. It was as difficult for her to talk as it was for me to watch her try.

"Who was it?"

"Doct-" The word cut out as she winced in pain. Whatever he had used on her was tearing her insides apart. I told her I could get her help, but she shook her head. "Too far. Won't make it. Just promise..."

"Of course I will."

She smiled again. "It's so nice to see your eyes." Suddenly her smile twisted and she began spasming underneath me. Her body bounced violently up and down, arms and legs slapping hard rock, and I tried my best to hold her still, keep her from hurting herself, my body-weight pressed down on her. But soon the spasms stopped. Her eyes lost focus and she exhaled one, final, small breath.

Right there, in my hands, my sister died. I allowed myself a moment before my thoughts turned to the good doctor, the man who had promised to give me my life back and ended up taking it from me. As I pictured his face, I became aware of the cave around me growing brighter, the body of another guard now visible, the ocean water where it entered the cave, all of it cast in blood red.

The machine on my chest, it fed on my anger. The hotter I burned the hotter it did, until the cave was like the head of a struck match. As fast as my remembering limbs would take me, I climbed the ladder and exited the cave, emerging into the dark woods which had been my home for too long. Before I left I shut the door behind me and made sure it was properly concealed by the plants and ivy and other things that grew there.

Like a searing flame I crossed the island. The old trees lit up in my presence. I ignored everything except my destination. Even as I came alive with fresh senses I thought of one thing only, one man. Like the coward he was, I knew I would find him near the dock trying to escape the consequences he deserved. Not twenty yards from the buildings near the dock, I heard his wretched voice.

"I didn't say twenty minutes, I said thirty." Through the trees I could see him, standing in the clearing, arguing with a man on the phone. "You can justify it however you want, but if your brother isn't pulling up to this dock in thirty minutes, it will be your head. Do you understand me?" He had been stabbed, the back of his coat slick with blood. I hoped it was my sister who'd done the deed, but I had the faint memory of it in the back of my mind, as if I'd done it myself.

I waited for him to hang up the phone before I stepped out from the trees. The sound of my foot breaking a twig caught his attention, and his hand tensed around his gun. He relaxed when he saw it was me, as if I didn't pose a threat. "Get back to the lab," he ordered. Like I was his dog.

"I saw what you did to her."

The doctor's face tensed up as he reevaluated my presence. "It was unavoidable," he concluded, "now help me with him so we can finish this." He looked over to the small guard building, through the door which seemed to be blocked from the inside. "There, he sees me," the doctor said, "now is the time."

"If I help you with him, you help me with her."

He looked back at me. "You're mad."

"Yes. I am." I walked slowly toward the doctor, and for the first time since I met him, fear crossed his eyes.

"I told you it was unavoidable. Even if I wanted to, there isn't enough to time to bring her back." As he babbled and fumbled over his words, I took hold of the metal contraption wrapped around my chest and began to pull it from my skin. I ignored the pain of the needles and wires ripping free. "Now hold on, the body doesn't give up the old spirit so easily. You're only half in this world!" I tore the remainder of the machine off my body and advanced on him, wielding it above my head as a weapon. He stepped back and tripped over a large root, falling on his back.

"Help me," I said.

"Of course," he replied. He raised his gun and fired. The bullet screamed past my ear.

The rage exploded in my chest as I began to bludgeon him with his own device. "There's still work to be done," he screamed, firing again, but I could barely hear him, my ears gone deaf. Not wanting to break the contraption, I threw it aside and choked him with my hands, and even as the bulb dimmed, all was red in the night.

With my lungs burning I left him there and began working on the office door, beating against it with my hands and body. A shout came from inside the small building. I beat on it harder until the wood cracked, and after a minute I pushed it the rest of the way open.

A stitched together man stood frantically typing at the computer. He wore guard's clothes and the parts of a dozen, different corpses- a suit which had recently belonged to me. The patchwork man looked at me, at my face, and a look of familiarity filled his eyes, followed by horror.

"What," he exclaimed. He looked down at his hands. Turned them over to see the black thread holding them together. "No! You can't!"

Using his disorientation against him, I attacked the patchwork man. We fought brutally, each of us laying claim over the same earthly body, and at times I saw the struggle from his eyes, and at times I could feel him seeing it through mine, but his weak, assembled body was no match for mine. He managed to bruise and cut my new face, but in the end I was the one left standing.

As his mismatched eyes grayed over, I read the screen to see what he'd been so passionately writing.

"Listen, I'm writing this because I have no phone and no one to email. My father is dead and my mother might as well be. I have no friends and no one to help me. Don't come out here, I'll update tomorrow. I'll be okay. I'll think of something. God, just don't come out here. Before I sign off, I have something to confess. I wasn't just hired to be a guard. That was how it started, but then it became something more. These men approached me and said the doctor was conducting secret studies on the island. They said he'd discovered the soul. The man with the birthmark, he told me the doctor made a breakthrough in something called Spirit Retrieval. That they wanted me to spy on him, to get it for themselves, or they'd tell people what I did. That I was responsible for my father's death."

"I didn't believe it at first but now I think the island is some kind of focal point. Stealing the body parts, that's just phase one. Once they get the spirit into the body it can be transferred into someone whole. Someone alive. That red glow out there, whatever killed the doctor, I think it's the brother, and I think I know what he wants. If I make it off this island, that is if my body makes it to shore, it might not be just me inside of it."

"Whatever you do, don't trust me."

With one, bloody finger I held down the backspace key until I was satisfied, then hit Send. I stripped the patchwork man of his uniform, put it on myself, and dragged his body into the woods to join the others. Let the sniveling men deal with it, the men who sniffed and pried and stole for themselves. Like so many maggots I'd come to know.

As I stood at the end of the dock to wait for the boat, the sting of the wind on my damaged body, I could feel the guard inside, fighting me, the patchwork man struggling to take his life back. He didn't understand the futility of his fight, for the simple reason that I wanted it more, his life, his vessel, and would do more to keep it. It was that simple- I would pull his strings until it was time to cut them.

You won't hear from me after today. You will never see me again. I will not tell you where I am or where I'm going. This is my final transmission.

One day, I'll come back for her.

About the Author

Brian Martinez has been known to watch a John Carpenter movie on repeat until people grow concerned. A certified Horror nut, he studied Film at Long Island University. He currently lives in New York with his wife Natalia and their pack of crazy dogs.

Martinez is known for numerous apocalyptic works including A Chemical Fire, The Mountain and The City, and the Bleeders series. He also writes The Vessel, a Space Horror podcast on all major platforms. His works have appeared on screen and in print, as well as on Youtube and in audiobook. He is currently working on The Unseen, a major, multi-character Supernatural Thriller series.

Learn more at http://www.bloodstreamcity.com

More by Brian Martinez

A Chemical Fire

Kissing You is Like Trying to Punch a Ghost

De-Partment

The Mountain and The City

The Vessel

Bleeders: Book 1, The Red Death

Bleeders: Book 2, A Rising Storm

Shallow Graves: The Unseen, Book 1

City of Demons: The Unseen, Book 2

www.ingramcontent.com/pod-product-compliance
Lightning Source LLC
Chambersburg PA
CBHW031341160726
47993CB00002B/788